Revenge for Janie

Revenge for Janie

A Ross Hendershot Novel IV

H. Berkeley Rourke

Revenge, it is said, should be served cold.
But life taken cries out for equally
cruel results to those of the killer,
doesn't it?
But who takes the revenge?

Contents

1

Ross and Ralph Ride to Yuma

October 1910

Two men rode toward Yuma. It was deep into the year 1910. The men's names were Ross Hendershot and Ralph Forney. Though they had not seen each other in quite a while and had much to talk about they rode silently. Their horses were basically in charge of their trip, it being the horses who determined the gait at which they proceeded. It was the horses, within the constraints of an occasional movement of the reins under which they proceeded, which determined the direction, and it was the habits of youth leading the two men to engage in a mostly silent trek during the daylight hours of riding.

Talking took too much energy, each of them would say, if asked. Their way, the laconic, the quiet trust in their horses, the knowledge it was unnecessary to engage in conversation which certainly would come later, was the way of their lives, their experiences, their friendship of so many years standing. For each of them any extended discussion of the reason for their trek was a little painful, and it needed some time for them to mull it over before letting words flow.

Each had started his journey separately and the journey had proceeded in a solitary way for at least a couple of days. Their trail had joined in the early morning as the shafts of the son dawning slowly in the east found its way over the desert mountains. As they rode toward each other, seeing each other from afar at first, each thought of the many times they had ridden together in the past. It seemed to each of them as though those times had occurred in other lifetimes, or maybe just a few days in the past. They were both old enough to realize in a way the idea of other lifetimes was true, but time passing would not change their enjoyment of being together again.

They stopped as their horses came near to each other. They dismounted, walked to each other and in the familiar way of the Mexican people, embraced. As they did each wiped away a tear without embarrassment and then smiled. Ralph said, "Good to see you Ross."

Ross said "Helluva way to get us back together again, but it's good to see you too Ralph. Come on any pilgrims on the way?" Ross's was asking if Ralph had run into any problematical persons on his ride to the point where they met.

"Nah." Ralph said. "A few Yaquis on their way south, nothing troublesome though. How about you?"

"No. I was hoping to run onto the Martin kid and truss him up to the back of a horse," Ross said, grinning broadly, "and take him back with you, and end this thing early. But I guess it's not to be, so let's get on with it."

They mounted, gave the horses their head and started west again. They walked the horses, eating the distance a few feet at a time. The first few miles after meeting led to some conversation about how long it had been, what their wives had said to each of them about the trip, and a very brief discussion about the reason they were riding together again. Their laconic nature, the fact they were more men of action than talk, meant a question such as, "How is Flora?", from Ralph, brought an answer of "She's just fine, said to say hello."

The talk waned and finally died altogether as they rode. The initial thoughts each held about the trek were enough to know and justify their journey. Neither needed or wanted to discuss much more than those few words which passed. More would come later. It could wait. Neither was anxious to discuss chasing down another running murderer. For Ralph, it was extremely close to his heart since in the first instance of the two men chasing down a rapist murderer, his daughter was the victim. Now Ross was placed in a very similar position.

Their trek would take several days and they were in arid country. The desert was dry, without rain for many months, was dusty, a foreboding presence to both men and their horses. Slow movements were not only necessary but appropriate to conserving the moisture in their systems. Part of the reason for not carrying on a long conversation was talking wasted moisture from their bodies. They carried skins of water for their horses and canteens for themselves.

The canteens could also be used for the horses if need be. If the men needed it a little water would be sipped, or mixed with a little pemmican as they rested the horses in the heat of the day. They would rather be thirsty themselves than have the horses go without sufficient water. The most water either of the men would use on the ride would be to make coffee in the morning before dawn and a small drink before going to sleep at night.

The horses were their life, after all. If the horses died so did they, and both were completely aware it was so. The arid conditions led them to stop every couple of hours, walk with the horses for a while, put some water in their hat and let the horses drink. It was stopgap at best but it would get them across the hot and the arid Sonoran landscape to San Luis Potosi'. The Sonoran Desert is cruel, hot and unforgiving. It is also sparsely covered with vegetation. There is creosote aplenty but only a few Mesquite or Palo Verde trees.

There were no trails to be followed on their trek. There was only the sun at their back in the morning and in front in the afternoon, and of course the horses. The horses were experienced, had worked the desert on their respective ranches, many times. They plodded along, avoiding the very soft areas, areas where holes had been dug by the likes of kangaroo mice. They also avoided the center pieces of the creosote bushes, knowing, as did the riders, there were sharp edges to be found there, edges which could cut the fetters of the horses with strong potential for infection to follow.

The men hoped, as they came together, to reach the small town of San Luis Potosi', Sonora, Mexico by evening. In time, as they rode both trusted they would encounter a trail, probably a north south leading trail. It would lead them to a hacienda or perhaps directly to San Luis Potosi' or some other obscure desert community. They thought San Luis to be about a day's ride from where they had met each other. It turned out to be closer to two day's riding. In San Luis, they would seek out the Alcalde, the mayor, who both knew very well, and see where it would be best to stay for the night. From San Luis, it still was about a two-day ride to Yuma, still across the difficult and dangerous desert. As the two men were going about setting up a camp they would for stay in for the night both prepared to discuss the day, the ride, the reason for the ride, the main topic they needed to talk about before the end of the evening.

As the sun began to glow yellow in the west, sinking slowly behind the hills it spread an array of colors across the sky. By then camp was set, some pemmican was being chewed on, and in time a smoke would hang out of the mouth of each. Admiring the golds, the purple hues, the fiery reds reflecting from the few scudding clouds, they stared, both missing their wives, ate their pemmican, some hardtack and drank a few sips of water. Before nightfall they gathered what wood they could find in this barren desert for a small fire. As they began to talk the embers of the fire blazed brightly. By the time their conversation was done the embers were all but extinguished.

They were riding to Yuma to meet with Ross's son, and Ralph Forney's godson, Ralph Manuel Hendershot, who they called Manny, and to attend the funeral of Manny's wife, if they arrived soon enough. She had been shot to death in what was a failed attempt to kill Manny. The deed was done by a man who came out of the dim recesses of Ross and Ralph's past. The man from the past was a son of another Ross had killed in the desert. The shooter's name was Robert Martin and Martin was on the run.

Martin left Yuma in a hurry after shooting Manny's wife. Ross, Ralph and Manny, and Ralph's son Jonas, also Ross's godson, would meet in Yuma to try and decide a way find Martin, to capture him and hopefully take him back to Yuma for a trial. Jonas and Manny had been in Yuma together as partners in The Palace Hotel for years. No one they knew had come forward to say with certainty where Martin had gone. Jonas and Manny were determined to find him, and so were Ralph and Ross.

In his youth, Jonas had worked for the U.S. Army as a tracker in southeastern Arizona Territory. He had participated in the recapture of several Apache leaders who, from time to time, fled the confines of the reservation. Their need to hunt, to gather horses from those who had them, in Mexico or the U.S., to battle with the Mexicans or Americans was almost a genetic trait. His job was to help the army track them down and bring them back to the reservation. He was a veteran of several skirmishes with Apache warriors, and had taken life in those fights.

He left home shortly before his seventeenth birth-day, not long after his mother passed away, and went to work for the Army as a mere lad. His education included harsh treatment by soldiers, settlers and na-tives as well. Eventually he tired of the cycle of drink-ing, fighting, collecting wages at the start of each month and beginning the cycle again. His timing was fortuitous because Ralph and Ross were ready to re-tire from the operation of the Palace. He took to the business operation, being trained by Ross, Flora and Ralph, like a duck to water, and operated the place with help from Manny. For several years Jonas had worked together with Manny, as partners, operating the Palace Hotel and Saloon. If Ralph and Ross could not depend on Jonas to be the tracker they would ask if Manuel Esquerra, a foreman at Ross and Flora's ranch, felt well enough to work with them again, but they fully expected Jonas to be with them.

Both Ross and Ralph had been living in Sonora, Mexico since 1908. Both had longed to work the land for many years. Ross and his wife Flora owned a small ranch on which they ran a few head of cattle and farmed several exotic crops Flora decided might flourish in Mexico. As she thought it would happen, when water was applied to the soil of their ranch, it would grow almost anything. Ross and Flora grew some melons they sold in the Mercado (marketplace) of the little town they lived in southeast of San Luis Potosi', Sonora, Mexico, ran some range cattle, and grew many other small crops.

They grew asparagus, a strange desert crop to say the least, along with some corn. The asparagus, which was more like a weed than a garden plant, once started was difficult to kill. They loved it in salads, pan fried or steamed. There were many ways to cook it. The garden bearing the asparagus was not large enough to grow a sufficient amount to sell, but it grew enough for them to eat, and to be able to give some to their campesinos and vaqueros (workers on the ranch). The campesinos thought Ross and Flora strange when it came to the asparagus, but their thoughts didn't stop them from eating it given the opportunity. With a little freshly churned butter it was superb and a fine staple to the normal diets of all on the Rancho Flora.

Ralph and his wife, Carmella, lived in Sonora as well, but a little farther south than Ross and Flora. They too ran a herd of cattle, slightly larger than Ross and Flora kept, and sold part of their herd in Hermosillo, the capital of the state of Sonora, every year. Occasionally they provided beef to some of the forces of Pancho Villa during the initial stages of the revolution which racked Mexico for so long. They grew basic corn crops which provided food for their campesinos and vaqueros. Ralph and Carmella paid fair wages to their campesinos as well as their vaqueros (meaning wranglers more or less). Both Ralph and Carmella were well respected by the people of the area in which they lived, largely Yaqui natives and their descendants, and were left alone by all the revolutionaries. Ross and Flora lived far enough away from the cities to be immune from the influences of the warring factions in the revolution.

The early conversation as the two met on the trail once again was all about Manny and his wife Janie. Ross, never a bitter man, was saddened by her death. Ralph, having encountered tragedy in the life of his first wife and his daughter, was more inclined to be angry toward the Martin boy. Both Ross and Ralph had something of an interest of their own in the capture of the Martin lad. Ross had killed the boy's father many years in the past. Ralph had killed the boy's uncle.

The boy's father had been a ne'er do well Robert had never known. Ross killed the man while on a trek to Yuma in 1878. The elder Martin had robbed a stage, had his horse shot and was seeking to steal all Ross's "possibles" including Ross's horse. Ross had been a better shot than Martin. Later, after two failed attempts to kill Ross in Welton and in the desert between Welton and Yuma, Ralph had killed the boy's uncle when the uncle was about to kill Ross. The shooting occurred in Yuma when, at the time, Ralph was Sheriff of Yuma County. Robert, before shooting Janie, had tried to assault Manny and failed, but threatened Manny based on the killing of his father and his uncle voicing a desire for revenge.

Ross and Ralph were dressed very similarly. Each wore dark trousers which defied a name or a label, not denims but perhaps a wool blend. Both men wore a light-colored shirt, and though perhaps at one time the shirts had been white, repeated use and repeated washing had created some off-white color tinged during their ride with brown as the dust kicked up by the horses imbedded itself into the fabric.

Both wore a vest with nothing in its pockets. Both wore what could have been a suit coat at one time, dark in color but heavily colored by the time they reached the area of San Luis Potosi' in the dust of the trail. Both wore a duster which had long ago lost its color of white and settled into something close to the color of the desert. Both sported wide brimmed hats keeping most of their face and neck shaded much of the day.

Both men rode loosely, comfortably, in the saddles they had occupied for what seemed most of their lives. Both men were weighted with pistols which, in part, long ago they had taken from others whose missions against them failed. Ross still carried two Colt Peacemaker pistols which he had taken from the body of George Martin, in fact.

They did not expect any trouble, but if it came they were still more than able to deal with it even though both were getting a little long in the tooth at sixty-eight years of age. Though guns worn openly were unusual in those changing times they thought them necessary in the circumstances. Whatever restrictions they might encounter in San Luis Potosi' or Yuma they would deal with when they arrived in those communities. Both carried at least one rifle in scabbards mounted along the right side of their horse's bodies.

Ross carried two rifles. One was a fifteen shot Henry repeating rifle and the other was a Sharps single shot rolling block fifty-six caliber buffalo gun which was accurate to well over five hundred yards. The Sharps was equipped with a scope and a tripod for long range shooting. Ralph carried his own Henry repeating rifle. There were more modern weapons available to either of them if they had chosen to acquire newer guns, but those they carried had been dependable in the most dangerous of circumstances. Neither saw any reason to look to the more modern "automatic" pistols seemingly so popular. Both carried so called "hideout" guns in special holsters in their boots. These were two shot Derringers which many men and women had carried throughout the history of the west.

There was no talk among them about the weapons they carried. Even though it was 1910 it was as natural for these men to carry guns and rifles as it was for them to breathe. They both had been born in northeast Texas in a time when revolution and war with natives was commonplace. The little youth they were given had more to do with monthly incursions by Comanches and the war of aggression (Civil War elsewhere) than it did with anything else. Hand guns and rifles, were an extension of their personalities, always with them, always on them.

Their lives had never known a time after about year ten when weapons had not been carried. Nothing had changed for them about the need to be armed in wild country. There were still bandits roaming the deserts of the Southwest and even an occasional wild and free native would go on a rampage. Though they did not expect to use the weapons for anything, except maybe to kill some game for a meal, they were prepared to and both were fully capable of using them to devastating effect in any situation.

There was no talk among them about what would happen when and if they finally captured the Martin boy. Either he would die or he would be brought back to Yuma to face a judge and a jury. They both would prefer he be captured and brought in front of a jury. They had no desire to kill the boy. Manny might feel, most likely did feel as though he would want the young man dead, but they had not spoken with Manny yet. The passage of time would bear answers to their questions, their unknown future.

In a sense, it was not really their fight, except it was their son and godson who had been wronged by the actions of the young Martin boy. Because Martin had shot at Manny, killing Manny's wife and unborn child, they were ready and willing to do anything they could to bring about justice in the situation. In the first instance justice meant to them the boy should be captured and put into the Arizona State Prison, but they would wait until they arrived in Yuma to decide the issue, if it could be decided.

Neither Ross nor Ralph thought of their trek to help Manny as being an assignation with revenge in any sense at all.

The country through which they rode, the northern part of the Sonoran Desert, was very dry, had very few trees, little or no shade sufficient to stop in and rest their animals. They took breaks, they gave the animals water and a little feed they had brought with them. They traveled lightly, with a rope tied to the pommel of the saddle with a pigging string. They had a bedroll on behind the saddle and saddlebags that carried necessary items like ammunition, jerky, hardtack, pemmican, some grain for the horses, some changes of socks and underwear and a few items to be used for drinking coffee or eating if they managed to shoot some game along their way.

They walked with the horses from time to time to rest them to a degree. They sat in the shade of a tree with the horses if one became available and let the horses graze on anything which was edible around the tree. These horses were accustomed to their riders, and the horses were accustomed to being treated well out on the range. The respect and care they took of their horses was second nature to both.

The nature of the country they traveled through would not change again until they crossed the U.S. border and headed toward Yuma. The trip could be shortened a bit when they went into the U.S. by cutting across the badlands between the Colorado River and Yuma, but they would stay close to the river bank to enhance their water supply for the horses. It would lengthen the ride by about a day but theirs was a trip with no time requirements. Even though the trip was brought about by an unspeakable tragedy in the murder of Janie the desert, the necessities of care being given to and used with their animals did not change.

There was no urgency in the notes they had received, no sense imparted their arrival needed to occur within the speediest time possible. Had there been a message to hurry as fast as they could they would have ridden to Tombstone and caught a stage which would take them across the desert from station to station. Even then the likelihood of their arriving in Yuma prior to the burial of Manny's wife was not very high. Yuma was far enough away from where both Ralph and Ross lived so no rapid basis existed for the two of them to get to Yuma.

Manny and Jonas needed time to ready the business of the Palace Hotel and Saloon for their absence under any circumstance. Ross and Ralph knew setting up the business to enable the pursuit of Martin was a necessity since they had run the same establishment in years past. Aside from the reasons for their trek they were enjoying the chance to spend time together in a peaceful moment of their lives. Many of the times they had shared in the past were tumultuous, enjoyable but fraught with danger in most cases.

Both Ross and Ralph were 68 years of age, but neither appeared to have worn his years badly. Both appeared to be and in fact were in good health. Both were tall men. Ralph was near to six feet in height and Ross was slightly taller at about six feet two inches tall. The years had never caused them to stoop or bend over. Neither of them carried much more weight at 68 than they had at 35 or 40 in the times when they first met.

Their faces were weathered to be sure. There were lines which had grown deeper and longer as the years passed, but both men appeared, except for a few additional lines in their faces, to be much younger than their actual years. These were hard men in exterior, hard men in response to being personally attacked, but men of great emotion, who held great love for those in their families.

Both had worked hard on their ranches and the hard work had kept them younger in health if not in their faces. Neither felt their age a hindrance of any kind as it related to the task at hand, or anything else. Neither of them really thought about their age much if truth be told. They were men, they were older men now, but they were not useless men or men who could not perform any kind of service which might be needed. They both reckoned themselves to be very fortunate not to have gotten sick at any point in their lives.

There was a time in Texas just before each of them was born in which cholera had taken a huge toll of the population. Through the years both had lived there were mini-epidemics of cholera, a dread disease which would take some from almost every family. Their families were struck from time to time but neither Ross nor Ralph had ever

contracted a serious illness.

The little bit of conversation they had as they rode was mostly centered on what their sons had been doing with their lives and how well the women were, the women they discussed being Carmella and Flora, their wives. Neither chose to talk much about himself as was in keeping with their lifetime habits. Ross said, "Flora told me I was getting a little long in the tooth for this kind of trek, Ralph. Did Carmella give you the same kind of static?"

"No, she was not really happy to have us have to do this, but she was pretty clear it was not going to be something either of us were too old to get involved in. She knows you work just as hard at your place as I do mine. Because of our having to work so hard this is like a vacation in a way. When the note came from Jonas I started packing stuff up and she was surprised. After she read the note she didn't say another word except to ask where you and I would try to meet each other. When I told her it would be somewhere between San Luis and the house she asked how long it would take me to get there. I said probably about two days ride. She nodded and started putting away some food for me."

"We had a man come from Nogales south to let us know," Ross said. "The sheriff in Nogales got a telegraph from the sheriff in Yuma and asked a guy to ride down and let us know. Did you hear anything from Jonas as to how Manny was taking the whole thing, Ralph?"

"Nothing was in the note except Jonas mentioned Manny was broken up over it. I guess his reaction was to be expected though. A hard thing, this." Ralph didn't have to add to his comment because Ross had been there with him when his lifetime had been filled with the tragedy of his daughter, at age fourteen, being raped and murdered. The murder of his daughter and its consequences had led the two of them on long rides together in the past.

"It sure brings back some memories for you I would guess," Ross replied.

"Yeah," said Ralph, "and some of them I would rather not have had to bring up again frankly, but given everything it's good that we are going to help the boys. I don't know if both can get away from the business at the same time, but if Jonas can't go what do you think about trying to bring Manuel Esquerra up from your ranch to help us with this?"

"I was thinking about him just a little while ago, Ralph. When Flora hired him to work for us it was one of her greatest decisions. He is a marvel around the ranch and can really run it without me or Flora there if the need arises. I am sure she can do that as well. If the need arises when we get to Yuma we can send a wire to Nogales and have it delivered to our ranch just like they did to tell us about Janie being killed. But you know Ralph it might be best if I leave Manuel there to run the ranch and bring Flora up to Yuma to take over the Hotel and Saloon while you and I, Manny and Jonas go after this one."

"Well I guess we will be able to figure it out when we get to Yuma, pard. Let's get some rest. Tomorrow should not be a long day but then you never know out here do you? By the way, Ralph, do you know who is the sheriff in Yuma now? I wonder if he has your same rules about wearing guns?" Ross thought it was probably a stupid question. He didn't really expect Ralph to answer. Ralph did not. The rest of the trek to Yuma was uneventful.

There was a lot of silence, a lot of memories which Ralph really didn't want to rehash as they rode, and a lot of concern and care about Manny in Ross's mind. There was some aches and pains which might not have existed in the past on similar long rides, or which maybe were simply forgotten. There were some creaking joints, and carping about them by both, in the mornings, and recognition those things had never occurred in past rides of a similar nature. There were a lot of smiles, some laughter at themselves, and then as they remembered the reason for being where they were, momentary frowns.

2

1910 Yuma

By 1910 the town of Yuma had grown in population, the number of people living there growing to almost 3,000 souls. The population was more than double what it had been when Ralph, and then Ross, first came to the town. In 1877 the railroad bridge across the Colorado River was completed. Ft. Yuma still was in existence in 1910 but it was no longer a necessity to the protection of the residents of the town. There was a spur line which went into Phoenix from Yuma and one could travel to San Diego by railroad as well.

Irrigation of the verdant farmland along the east banks of the Colorado River running back more than twenty miles to the confluence with the Gila had been made possible by the installation of the Siphon. Water pulled from the Colorado enabled the growing of many kinds of cash crops. Farming was rapidly, in 1910, becoming the predominant economic activity in Yuma. The soil deposited from the floods of the Colorado for many hundreds of years was rich and loamy, and it was discovered it would grow anything. Even exotic vegetable crops began to be harvested in the valley.

The river traffic which had flourished in the past taking mostly copper ore out to the ships, but with some gold and silver as well, was reduced by the many sandbars in the Colorado River. The lack of a need for ships carrying cargo in the Sea of Cortez bound for Arizona and California inland towns also made inroads in the river business. In the past river lorries, called "lighters," had traveled from the mouth of the Colorado upriver bringing goods in exchange for ores mined all over the state of Arizona as well as goods to be transshipped by stagecoach or wagon eastward and westward to inland Arizona and California communities. The usage of more and more water from the Colorado and the damming of the river with a weir near Blythe and a dam near Yuma was instrumental in reducing the boat traffic on the Colorado. The Laguna Dam was completed in 1909 north of Yuma which also meant the Yuma valley, always subject to the whims and floods of the formerly uncontrolled Colorado River, was less likely to be flooded at least once a year. Before the dam was built the Colorado, mostly peaceful and calm, would rage with turbulent flood waters at least once a year and sometimes more often, and leave the entire area through which it ran sodden and muddy. No longer would the floods come annually in Yuma after 1909.

Yuma, a name deriving from the Quechan native language, was becoming civilized. Well, it was becoming civilized to the degree any town in Arizona was in 1910. There were no symphonic orchestras in Arizona in 1910, no art centers, no museums of natural history. Men and women still, on many occasions and depending on where they worked throughout the state, carried guns with them wherever they went and sometimes solved human problems with their guns.

Though the day of the use of a gun in the normal societal settings as a problem resolving tool was waning in Yuma, it was not dead. There were also men, and women, whose use of the gun made them criminals, whose morality concerning guns was nonexistent, men like the Martin boy. The last of the incidents of a shootout by a posse with "rustlers" had taken place not too long before Ralph and Ross began their ride near Prescott. Arizona.

These people, the criminal element, cared not about the development of "society" in Arizona. They placed no credence in the idea that an art museum could flourish in an Arizona city. Their desires in terms of the "growth of their city" might be more akin to how many places in the town served alcoholic beverages. Or it might be how many whorehouses were there in the town.

Stand in the way of one of these "criminals" who was holding a gun and it was certain you *could* get shot, though not if you *would*. If the man or woman wielding the weapon was a good shot, a rarity by comparison to the content of the pulp "western" stories of the day, then you might get killed. There were far fewer men who carried guns in Yuma, and in Arizona in general by 1910. The Arizona Territory was trying to become the 48th state of the union. In part, the fact statehood was being sought meant more law enforcement, stricter attitudes toward enforcement of bans on wearing guns in town, among other things. Robert Martin was one of those whose desires, whose attitudes, whose activities were more akin to those of the "old" Yuma, the Yuma of the time of the gunsel, those whose propensity to kill was much larger than their desire to see a wonderful singer perform. Robert was the bastard son of George Martin. He was completely amoral, totally without remorse for anything he did and consumed with his desire to kill one of those who had killed his kin.

Robert knew the stories well. He knew his father was a stagecoach robber and his father had been being chased by a posse out of Welton when Ross Hendershot killed George. He also knew the story of his uncle being killed by Ralph Forney. He didn't care if it was Ralph or Ross he killed, or Manny Hendershot or Jonas Forney. He simply had a yen to kill one of the family members of those hated bastards who had gunned down his father and uncle.

George Martin, Robert's father, grew up in Yuma along with his brother William. George was a ne'er do well, a thief as a boy, a rustler as a man. His cattle thieving was likely to get his neck "stretched" if ever he was caught so mostly it took place at night when he could gather one steer or bull or cow from a herd or from the brush where the cattle often lived. The animal would be butchered, its hide buried or burned, its bones were not used with the meat and were burned or buried as well.

George cared not if the steer wore a brand or was an unbranded brush popper. It was not out of desire he took the cattle, it was out of need more than anything. His family was extremely poor. The fact

George never really tried to get a steady job of any kind was, in part, responsible for his family's plight. So was the booze George liked too well and consumed in large quantities all too often.

George Martin was born of a woman of ill repute and a drover who was passing through town. His father was gone within a few days, never to return, never to be known by his son. George's mother paid him little heed and especially after she had a second son by another drifter. George's youth was largely a function of his own choices once he grew beyond the stage of infancy. Even as a toddler in nappies he was seen playing in the dirt outside bars where his mother was turning tricks. Since she was not a woman blessed with a great figure or a beautiful face she worked the cribs and the rough bars of Yuma's mean streets. She never worked in the Palace.

The father of the second son stayed for a time but he could see her ways were set and he didn't particularly want to share her with anyone much less four or five men a day, and more on some days. She worked all day every day as a prostitute and earned damned little at her work. She was required to pay for the usage of a room in the cribs she worked, and she too was given to drinking too much booze, with the result she brought little home to enable her feeding her children.

George and his brother "raised" themselves in a very real sense. After William's birth both were often seen in the dirt outside saloons in which their mother worked as a prostitute. They were not more or less noticeable than the other urchins who played alongside them. As one might expect the experiences of their youth led George and his brother William to be on the seedy side of the law all their lives.

George's sense of the appropriate and inappropriate was very poorly developed because of such intermittent or non-existent parenting during his childhood. The same attitudes were well set in his brother's head. George, in fact, had little to do with his brother most of the time and preferred it to be true as the two of them grew up beyond the toddler years. As he grew into his teen years and began to be able to use the services of women who worked in the same profession as his mother he wanted even less to do with his brother.

George was possessed of a sense of desire to achieve but with no ability to accomplish his goal. He never attended school and he never really learned a trade. As a small boy he watched the kids troop down the streets on their way to school, wondering what it was like. He was never to find out. He could not read or write, even as an adult. He had no envy of those who could read and write. He had his own way of living without education being a part of his meager existence.

By the time George Martin was six years old he worked in one of the saloons in which his mother toiled as well. By then she was drinking so heavily she seldom brought home any food. He learned if he wanted to eat he had to work. His first job as a boy of six years old was cleaning spittoons. By eight he had a better job working in one of the liveries in town in which he cleaned up after the animals. By eight he was big enough and strong enough to shovel horse manure into a wheel barrow and take it out of the stables.

He stole what he could not buy and that was almost everything he had. His paltry wages were not enough to be able to feed both he and his younger brother. He became adept at stealing an orange or an apple or even a potato if one were available in an open box in one of the "general stores" in Yuma. The proprietors of the stores Knew who was stealing from them and would complain loudly to the sheriff or a sheriff's deputy, knowing nothing would be done to remedy the behaviors.

George would run away from the proprietor of the store gleefully laughing as the owner gave chase. He always escaped, always could take an apple or something home for he and his little brother to split between them. In time, the owners simply chalked up the losses to their overhead and went on about their business. Even as George grew older and bolder there seemed to be nothing the law enforcement people would or could do to stifle his bad behaviors.

As he reached his teen years George began to try and steal things which had a little higher value. His efforts landed him in Sheriff Forney's jail, such as it was, a couple of times. The sheriff was nice to him though, and fed him when he was in jail. In those days his brother had begun to work and follow George's example so it was unnecessary for George to worry much about the kid. Both the Martin boys were small men which left them unable to be a mugger. Neither was particularly strong though they were both hard and lean in the time when almost all men looked similar.

By the time he was sixteen he was lucky to find a horse running wild on the desert, rope it, train it, and saddle it with the saddle of a deceased cowboy. The horse likely came from a native or was a mustang. It bore no brand nor earmarks so in a sense it was fair game for George. No one came along to complain the horse had been stolen. The fact he had his own horse gave him mobility but some independence though he did have to keep it in the stable. He persuaded the livery owner to allow him to stable the horse there for the moment by helping with the chores of the stables.

His last major acquisition was a pair of forty-five caliber handguns. On one of his frequent desert rides he saw a man who had died in the desert. He got to the man before all the man's possessions were either taken or ruined by the sun. He took the guns, along with several other things he salvaged from the man, and he began to range out away from Yuma to do his thievery. All who knew George felt strongly it was only a matter of time until he was an occupant of one of the cells in the new Arizona Territorial Prison built in Yuma in the year 1876. He really didn't care if he was in jail or not. Being in jail was okay if the guards were not cruel. At least in the jail he was fed every day.

Even though he roamed freely around Arizona, spending time in the new town of Phoenix, in Tucson and in Tombstone among other places, George came home every now and again. As luck would have it one starry night when he was being serviced by a new young lady of the night he impregnated her. At least she claimed it was George who had caused her to be with child. Since she was a prostitute there was a great question in his mind, but then again she identified him, and it seemed to him he needed to be responsible, to do the right thing for his child. It was probably the first time in George's unproductive and morally bankrupt life he made a decision based on what was responsible.

George decided he would try to do some honest work, try to take care of the woman and the child. He looked hard for a job in the town which would pay a sufficient wage for the two of them to live together without her continuing to service other men. They found a small parcel of land just out of town which was available and squatted on it. George had few skills which would enable him to make the place successful, but others took pity on him, some he called friends, and his brother helped as well.

It was not easy, not a beginning of a great loving relationship. Times were hard for everyone, but a home was built, a well was dug, a large stock tank was built, and a few head of cattle were gathered from the breaks which had no brands on them. He and his woman, knowing they could not make it completely without her participation, agreed she should work at least a couple of days taking care of some drovers who passed by on their way to nowhere.

They hung on by their teeth for a time. He sold the stock save for those the two of them and his younger brother ate. She worked a garden as much as she was able, but it just was not working for them. George left saying he would be back, knowing all the time he would never return. She knew he was gone for good, she never saw him again, but she really didn't care much. The baby was a burden, George was even more of a burden than the baby. She considered herself well shed of him when he left.

His drifting, thieving life, the life of an avowed ne'er do well, resumed. He got out of town, headed east and landed in Wellton, a very small community around forty miles east of Yuma. He worked a little in the saloon and whorehouse there but mostly he plotted how he could make a big score which would allow him to move on further east.

George decided to try and rob a stage which was on a run between Phoenix and Yuma. He waited until he knew what the rough schedule of the stage would be and then set up east of Wellton to stop it, rob whatever money it was carrying either from patrons or otherwise. The entire effort was a failure. The stage had no money and the men riding on it were hard men who shot back at George rather than be stopped. It was after his attempt at robbery in which George's horse was shot he and Ross Hendershot encountered each other in the desert outside of Welton. George tried to shoot Hendershot. He tried to sneak up on Ross, not knowing who Ross was, or caring.

He wanted Ross's horse and everything else Ross had along with the horse. He tried a ruse by dropping one of the pistols on the ground. But when he grabbed the other one from behind his back it all went wrong. He fired in Ross's direction and missed, while Ross shot back and did not miss. George died a lonely death in the desert and helped create hell for his woman and child by claiming he knew nothing of where they were. Ross was the kind of man who if he had known George had a child Ross would likely have given the woman some money at the very least, but the information was never shared with Ross.

Ross buried George there on the desert but a posse which had been chasing him coming from Welton met Ross, found out George was dead, found out where George had been buried, and brought George's body back to Welton. George was buried in Welton after Ross identified his body and the stage driver told Sheriff John George had been the one who tried to rob the stage. Ross claimed a hundred-dollar reward posted for George and eventually moved on to Yuma. George's son William began his hard row to hoe in the same fashion as his father but because his father was dead rather than simply being a deadbeat.

In Yuma Ross, befriended Ralph Forney right away. They met as Ross entered Yuma. Each drover or pilgrim who came into town realized right away firearms could not be carried openly in the town. A sign very like one posted in Dodge City, Kansas warned the new resident of the rules concerning wearing guns. In due course, or sometimes right away a deputy would contact a new potential resident and take him to see Ralph Forney about wearing guns. In Ross's case, the deputy saw him riding down the street and took him directly to the sheriff.

Ross respected the rule of law in general and certainly after meeting Ralph he respected Ralph's position as sheriff, and his attitude toward guns being worn on the streets of Yuma. Ross also met George Martin's younger brother William in the desert between Yuma and Welton. William was floated out of Welton by the sheriff there for making a drunken attempt to shoot Ross. The younger Martin tried later to "drygulch" him and failed. Eventually Ross let the younger Martin live and thought he had sent him on his way to the northern part of the state or maybe to California. But Martin came back to Yuma and made another attempt on Ross's life on the streets of Yuma.

William Martin would have been successful in killing Ross save for the presence of Ralph Forney. The sheriff shot and killed Martin. William slightly wounded Ross, who fell in the dirt, and as William advanced toward Ross to administer the coup de grace the sheriff came out of his office, saw William preparing to kill Ross and shot the younger Martin dead with a shotgun. The friendship between Ross and Ralph was cemented further.

In the run of time Ross and Ralph engaged in covering each other's backs in a gun battle, and were together in the task of chasing down the killer who had raped and killed Ralph's teen aged daughter when she was but fourteen. Ross, Flora and Ralph became business partners in the Palace Hotel, Saloon and Fancy House. Ross and his wife Flora, and Ralph and his wife Carmelita, had only retired from the operation of the business a few years prior to it being taken over by Jonas and Manny.

Manny was young, very young to be married and helping to run a hotel and saloon, but he and Jonas were successful, as had their parents been before them, even sending some cash to their parents on occasion. Then along came the forgotten son of George Martin. Robert Martin's life was anything but easy from the time of his infancy to the time of his early adulthood in Yuma. His mother essentially abandoned him to the whims of the Gods and all her friends working as prostitutes. He too cleaned spittoons, swamped saloons, scrubbed dirty sheets every day to make a few pennies for his mother, helping to fuel her consumption of booze.

The appearance of Robert Martin was not welcomed in Yuma by anyone. In time all would know

why he seemed such an outcast, such a negative influence in their community. The legacy of his father
and brother lived on. Having grown up as his father's
bastard son was a misfortune not only for William
but everyone he encountered in life.

3

Manny, Janie and Robert Martin

March 1910

Manny, whose full name was Ralph Manuel Hendershot, was a very callow young man of eighteen years who married his childhood sweetheart. He had loved her since she was but a child, and she felt the same about him. She was named Jane Mary Hart prior to marriage. Her parents came to Yuma to try and open a mercantile store. Janie's father, Monroe, went to work in the mercantile store owned by Flora Hendershot because of her inheritance from George A. Bonhomme.

Before the Hendershots left Yuma and moved into El Norte de Sonora she sold the mercantile store to Monroe for a very small price. She gave it to him for a song in recognition of his prior work there. His efforts to make the General Store successful thereafter brought him great happiness. During his time in Yuma he married and had three children, one of which was called Jane or more commonly Janie. Janie was a very lucky young girl in a way. She grew up with an older brother, and a younger brother, but no sisters. She wrapped her father around her little finger and he loved every minute of their special relationship. She grew up being indulged by her father, a very happy and precocious child whose loving nature was enhanced by the doting nature of her father's love for her.

Janie was small, only five feet two inches tall and never weighed more than about one hundred twenty pounds in her seventeen years prior to marriage. She was blond and blue eyed but possessed a creamy complexion which seemed to love the sun of Yuma and the desert. She always seemed to have a healthy glow about her regardless of the time of year. Her face was small, oval, and whether she was standing in front of another, or was being viewed in parallax, she was very pretty. Her looks were not a talisman for her though and no one, not her parents, not Manny, not any of her classmates held any feeling Janie was in love with her looks.

She was a bit sassy with her mother and father but honored their wishes in the end when the three of them disagreed about some topic of concern. Disagreements between them didn't often so if she had to give in on a position she didn't feel it was an imposition. She was not rebellious, just a pert, sassy, young and beautiful girl growing up in love. Sex was not something about which she wanted to think, even about having sex with Manny, until marriage occurred. Life was full of happy surprises for a smart and beautiful girl like Janie. She reveled in life, loved where she lived, loved her parents, loved going to church and loved God, and eventually loved Ralph Manuel Hendershot almost more than she could imagine.

Manny and Janie went to school together from their first to their last day of school. They learned to ride together, they learned about the desert and the river together. They learned how a kiss felt when for the first time for each, they kissed. They petted some, exploring a little in indirect ways, never pushing each other or engaging in anything they thought would lead to sex. Neither of them thought of a future without the other in their life after they entered their teen years. It was simply assumed by both they would marry and live happily ever after in Yuma.

They began to talk about marrying each other when they were only twelve years old. It seemed they were destined to be together as young adults and in time as husband and wife. At age seventeen Manny asked her to marry him and she agreed. It was an expectation more than a surprise to her parents and most of the people who knew anything of the two youngsters in Yuma.

They had, for a couple of years, both being teenagers, walked shoulder to shoulder, held hands regularly and publicly, could be seen sitting very close to each other in the new Methodist Church in town which they both attended every Sunday. In all but the sleeping hours they were inseparable. The preparations for the marriage were done almost exclusively by Janie's mother, Wilhemina, in no small measure because neither Flora nor Carmelita lived in Yuma during the time immediately before the wedding.

The ceremony, which Ross and Flora, and Ralph and Carmella attended, was beautiful and an event which brought about a torrent of tears among the women and a town wide celebration for days on end. Manny was handsome and in love. Janie was beautiful and in love. He was dressed in the typical black frock coat so ubiquitous in those times. She was dressed in a white outfit which showed her to be a curvaceous young woman and which enhanced her beautiful skin color. Even the Methodist minister who married the two of them leaked tears as he performed the rituals of the ceremony. It was an auspicious beginning to what could only be a magical existence for these two young people.

Everyone expected they would be producing gorgeous children every year starting within a year or so. Most envied them if truth be known. Manny was a very handsome young man in his wedding suit, and Janie, well Janie was simply gorgeous. Their love for each other was completely evident to all who saw them. Their smiles lit up the faces of many in the crowd, just as they did each other. After the wedding they had no reason to hide their feelings any longer and did not.

They walked arm in arm or with arms around each other wherever they went in the town. They kissed openly and regularly though they knew it was frowned upon by the so-called city fathers. No one thought they were doing any harm by the openness of their love. They didn't flaunt sex. They just indulged in their deep feelings for each other constantly.

Robert Martin was only recently arrived in Yuma from central California when Manny and Janie married. Robert's mother had toiled in the mining camps in places such as Nevada City as a prostitute until she died. He had worked the mines in Nevada City until he saved enough to buy a horse and a gun. He had heard the stories of the death of his father and uncle many times. He meant to avenge them both. His true hope was to kill both Ralph Forney and Ross Hendershot. But when he arrived in Yuma Robert found neither Ralph nor Ross still lived there. It became of no moment because their sons were running the Palace.

Monroe reduced the prices in his store a great deal to celebrate and share his happiness over the marriage of Janie and Manny with his customers, with the result he made more money than ever before. Jonas Forney, still unmarried but engaged, after a fashion, to a woman he met in Mexico, had taken over the operation of the Palace Hotel and Saloon and after the wedding Manny joined him in being responsible for the business.

Manny worked there for several years before marrying. He learned much and was more than ready by eighteen to help Jonas run the place. The two younger men had done away with the prostitution business. Jonas believed it was safer and more profitable to run the place as a hotel, restaurant and saloon. He was correct in his judgment and by the time Manny became old enough to understand the detailed operation of the business it was flourishing.

It was a backdrop to the life Janie and Manny would lead together. Ironically, he and Janie stayed in the same suite of rooms, with the same kind of wonderful service provided to them as Ross and Flora had used many years earlier. There was a lot of tittering and veiled laughter at the beginnings of Manny and Janie's time together by employees of the hotel. Some helped her bathe, taught her how to take care of the soreness deriving from constant sex in the first week or so of the marriage.

It was a grand time for them all, Manny and Janie of course, but all the employees, Jonas and his lady, everyone who came into the place asking about the newlyweds. For the employees of the hotel she was magical. Her disposition was always sunny, no matter the issue, and she never was condemnatory of anyone. She worked hard in the business herself, seeing to it the laundry was done of all the bar towels, sheets, pillow cases and the like from both the saloon and the hotel.

It was a short-lived honeymoon for them all, Manny and Janie, and for all those who grew to love her in a few short months. All those good moments, all the happiness of those around them was destroyed in a flash because less than six months later Manny's bride was dead at the hands of Robert Martin.

Robert grew up almost entirely in the Nevada City, Grass Valley, California area. His mother worked the saloons which would accept her as a whore for the miners. She was older than many of the whores and the years showed on her face and in her figure. Nonetheless she could work most of the time. His father was never an issue in his life. When his father walked away from the two of them there was never another contact between them.

After his mother passed away he was destitute, but some kindly folks helped him find enough work so eventually he saved enough to buy a horse and a gun. It took a long time. He, like his father, had no education, no skills, no trade to offer an employer. He did all kinds of odd jobs to survive, mostly in the saloons. But he also shoveled shit in the same way as his father in the stables of Nevada City. Once he acquired his horse and his pistol he knew what he wanted. He wanted revenge for the killing of his father and uncle. If he was asked why he thought it was necessary for him to have revenge against the Hendershot family he could not give a simple answer. His attitudes in everything he did were colored by this constantly and openly spoken desire to kill a Hendershot.

When Robert arrived in Yuma he tried to find out where Ross Hendershot and Ralph Forney were located. Everyone he asked told him to go to the Palace and ask either for Jonas or Manny, but every time Robert went to the saloon neither Jonas nor Manny was available. People in Yuma at the time were not able to carry guns on their person unless they were on their way out of town. Robert, would have been unable to do anything about meeting either Jonas or Manny under any circumstance except maybe to administer a beating to one or both, assuming he was able to fight well enough. Finally, one bright Saturday afternoon Robert found and met Manny, as it turned out, to his chagrin.

Ross had been, still was, a tall man. He had passed some of his height on to his son, Manny who was thin, at near to one hundred and sixty pounds constant weight, and at a height of six feet three inches. Though he was tall and thin Manny was also wiry and strong, and Manny was unafraid of much of anything. Fearlessness, or at least the appearance of fearlessness had been one of the most constant characteristics of his father and he had inherited the trait.

Ralph's son Jonas was a hard, lean, tall man himself. Jonas was just above six feet tall and carried a weight of near one hundred eighty pounds. Both Manny and Jonas worked hard physically as well as by using their knowledge. The fact the Palace was still the only saloon in Yuma in which a man could buy a cold beer created much work in and of itself. The kegs of beer which came from various places were heavy and large.

For Jonas it was no task at all to manipulate them with a small lift or to move them around by brute force. It was a little more difficult for Manny but more as a matter of lack of experience than anything. He certainly didn't lack the strength to move the kegs of beer or whiskey which had to be poured into bottles. The combination of fearlessness and strength, along with some experience gained as a young lad, made Manny formidable in terms of engaging in the sweet science of boxing.

Robert, finding Manny alone in the bar save for the barman behind the bar, asked if he could talk with Manny. The latter, being a more gregarious sort than his father agreed, ordered a couple of cold beers and a bottle of decent whiskey and the two of them sat down at a table in the saloon. Robert opened the conversation with a question about a potential job. "Do you ever need a bouncer in here Mr. Hendershot?"

"No, no we don't sir. We rely on the sheriff's office which is very close by to take care of anyone who needs rough treatment. But they are few and far between. We never hire a bouncer. I guess in a way it is kind of a family point of pride. Sorry."

Robert sipped his whiskey which Manny had bought, then chased it with a little of the delicious and very cold beer.

"Do you have any other positions open now Mr. Hendershot?"

"Well, sir I cannot say we do, Mr. Martin. But certainly, sir we would be willing to put your name down in our records and look you up should we have a position come open." Manny knew even though he was offering to look at Martin in the future the operation of the Palace was primarily by family. Those who were not family with Manny or Jonas were such longtime friends there was little difference between them and family.

Manny had been smiling and cordial with Martin during the entire meeting. There was no reason for Manny to be otherwise. It was, after all, a man seeking employment, or at least so it seemed. Then, with his last swallow of beer gone Martin stood rapidly, stepped forward toward Manny and punched at him, hitting Manny in the left shoulder area with a blow which drove Manny out of his chair and onto the floor. Manny was more surprised than stunned, didn't rise right away because he saw Martin drawing a pistol from a hideout pocket. Manny heard the barman yell at Martin and thought bullets were about to fly.

The barmen who worked the Palace Saloon were protective of their owners, most having worked in the Palace for many years. The man on duty seeing Manny going to the floor, brought out a short-barreled shotgun which carried two deadly loads and pointed it in Martin's direction. He yelled at the top of his lungs, "Hold it right there son," as Martin brought out a hideout gun from a boot holster. As Martin raised the pistol and cocked it the barman continued, saying "If you do not want to die right this instant mister, you better let go of your pistol. This here shotgun will blow you into a pile of shit."

Martin heard the clicking of the hammers of the shotgun being engaged and looked back over his shoulder. Sure as hell the gaping maws of the gun which appeared to him to be large enough to crawl inside, were pointed in his direction. Martin, seeing both barrels pointed at him knew he might get a shot off at Hendershot but he also knew he would die the same moment.

He dropped the Derringer on the floor. It was a small caliber anyway meaning there was no certainty even if he shot Hendershot death would follow. It was a woman's gun and had belonged to his mother.

Manny watched all these things unfold as Robert pointed the gun at him and then dropped it on the floor. He wondered, what the hell did I do to this guy making him want to kill me so badly. It is for sure he didn't come here, as he said, looking for a job.

Manny got up off the floor while the barman, named Jake, was pointing the shotgun at Martin. Manny had never seen Martin before but Manny did know the story of George and William Martin who had been killed by his father Ross and by his god-father Ralph many years earlier. He thought, before asking, crap if I had asked the right question earlier in the conversation I could have avoided all this mess. Manny asked Martin, "Are you related to either George or William Martin, sir?"

Martin who was ever the smart ass for he knew no other way, responded, "Of course I am you ass." The sneer in Martin's voice was evident to anyone nearby. He continued, saying, "Do you think I would punch your skinny little ass for nothing? George Martin was my father. And your father killed my father, Mr. Hendershot. You are mine, son of Ross Hendershot, you are mine, and I intend to kill you, mister. But I will have to do it a little at a time I guess." Then Martin made another mistake calculated on his lack of knowledge about the Hendershots and Forneys. He assumed that Manny's stature, the fact Manny was so thin, made him both a coward and unable to defend himself.

Manny was neither a coward nor unable to defend himself with his hands. In his growing up there had been many battles. He was constantly taunted about his mother being a whore and his father running a saloon and whorehouse. His ability to fight men of much larger stature grew as he grew in years. Manny was not large as a young man. When he was younger he was not nearly as tall as his father, but he was strong. His father taught him well about taking the advantage in a fistfight, and Manny was willing. He made Martin understand how willing when he smiled at Martin and said to him, "I'm the bouncer here Mr. Martin. If you would kindly remove yourself from these premises I will not be forced to give you a lesson in the art of fist fighting. Your choice, my man, but make it wisely." The quiet and gentlemanly way in which Hendershot spoke once again persuaded Martin he had a fop for an opponent.

Martin advanced on Manny as the barman put the shotgun away but when the barman smiled Martin thought he might have made a mistake. It was then Manny hit Martin with several blows which brought Martin to his knees. As Martin, dazed and confused, sat on his knees, Manny hit him two or three more times before Martin was on his back on the floor.

Manny turned to the barman and said, "If you would run over to the sheriff's office and get a deputy I will watch this guy until you get back." The barman found a deputy in the sheriff's office and returned before Martin fully regained consciousness. When the deputy came in with the barman Manny said to both, "Pour yourself a cold beer, boys. He is not going to be coming around right away I don't think, and if he does I can always persuade him to go back to sleep for a time again if necessary."

The barman smiled at Manny and said "I thought there for a minute he was going to simply leave, Boss. But like so many before him he made the wrong choice. I guess your reputation is not as widespread as we might have thought."

"Well maybe there will come a time when people will not try to take advantage of me but the time has not yet arrived Jake. I guess I will just have to make do until then." Manny and Jake both smiled broadly at his comment as did the sheriff. They all knew Manny's status as the "bouncer" was well known and respected by most in the community. There were not many who were willing to walk into the Palace and try Manny. Here was one who didn't know and obviously had no respect. But he had the start of a lesson given to him by a quiet young man. Unfortunately, as future events would disclose, the lesson was not well learned.

About the time they ended their conversation Martin began to stir on the floor. Manny turned to the deputy and said, "Are you done with your beer yet or should I put him to sleep for a little while longer?"

The deputy said "I would be much obliged if you would put him to sleep for a while longer Mr. Hendershot. If you could just put him out for a little while, I would sip another of these wonderful beers and then I can throw him on the back of my horse and take him to the jail." Manny took out a sap and tapped Martin once lightly behind the ear. Martin obliged them all and slept again. Martin was released from jail right away when he woke up the next morning and understood he had picked on the wrong young man. The sheriff also made it clear to Martin packing guns of any type in the town was not permitted. The sheriff told Martin that the usual punishment for the crime of packing a hideout gun was a floater out of town. He asked Martin, "Do you want to stick around here in Yuma, young man?"

When Martin nodded his assent the sheriff told him, "Do not mess with Manny Hendershot or Jonas Forney. Manny will beat the crap out of you any time he wants and as you already know he is fully capable of exactly what happened to you yesterday. Jonas is more likely to kill you with his bare hands, and he knows how to do it just as well as Manny knows how to fight. Count on what I have told you and leave the two of them alone. Do you get my drift?" Once again Martin nodded, harboring the thought in his mind simultaneously he would kill Forney or Hendershot some way, some day. The sheriff let him loose with his promise to stay away from either of them, and to stay away from the Palace.

Jonas Forney was born in 1875. His earliest years in Yuma with his mother and father and his younger sister were idyllic. Then, late in his fourteenth year a bug came along, got hold of his mother and just wasted her away to nothing before killing her. His father, Ralph, was devastated, drank too much, didn't take the best care of his kids sometimes, was a little rougher on the kids than he had been when his beloved Georgi had been alive. Both Jonas and Jenny knew he loved them and knew his lack of attention was due to his extreme grief over the death of his beloved Georgi. Both tried hard to find ways to help him shake his grief, to come back to himself, but for more than a year nothing worked.

When Ralph finally began to come out of it for good a couple of years had passed by. Ross Hendershot and Flora had been surrogate mother and father to Jenny and Jonas, but Jonas had many chores to do around the small Forney ranch every day. So did Ralph and in between the times when Ralph was so drunk he was sleeping or semi-comatose, Ralph helped Jonas. Ralph saw Jonas blossoming into a great young man, and Ralph also saw his son growing further away from him as Jonas went into his teenage years.

Jonas was fifteen when the Army started seeking his expertise as a tracker. By age sixteen Jonas was employed full time by the Army though he never joined up. He was deeply involved in the process of hunting down and corralling the last of the break-away groups of Chiricuahua and White Mountain Apache natives in the eastern and southeastern parts of the territory of Arizona. In the years he was working for the army, by eighteen, Jonas was a hardened man, had been involved in combat with the natives on several occasions, was very proficient with a rifle and even more so with a forty-five caliber Colt pistol.

He was a wiry young man, not carrying much weight. His looks resembled those of his father a great deal but for the fact he was a little shorter than his father. Jonas stood just about six feet tall if he stretched himself out, and he weighed a maximum of about one hundred eighty pounds at any given time in his young life. In the style of some Apache braves he kept his hair a little longer than most young men, letting it fall free on his shoulders, almost affecting the appearance of Wild Bill Hickock. As a tracker, and as a shooter either from foot or horseback he grew to be very able, earning the nickname with some of the army youngsters of "brave." They opined he was as brave as any Apache warrior and perhaps as skilled on a horse or as a tracker.

Weeks on end in the saddle or running alongside his horse in the fashion of the Apache, made him rock hard all over his body. His time in the Army also made him aggressive to a larger degree than most of the men of his time. His long mane of dark hair and his flashing dark eyes made him a favorite of the local girls, and especially several ladies of the night who kept themselves only for him on some days of the week in the cribs near to Ft. Lowell in Tucson. As the new century turned he was ready to abandon his nomadic existence as an army scout and return to Yuma. He did so without knowledge of Ralph and Ross's desire, and the desire of Flora and Carmelita to go into ranching.

Soon Jonas oversaw the entire operation of the saloon, hotel and fancy house. As Jonas began to put his own stamp of style and ability on the operation of the business Ralph and Ross moved to Sonora and began their lives together with their ladies, as Patrons in Mexico. Not long afterward, with the diminishment of the army fort near Yuma to practically nothing and the spread of farming as the most highly sought after economic activity in the area Jonas ended the operation of the fancy house.

He kept several of the women on who had no place to go and they became shills for the bar but not providers of sexual favors except to their male friends. None of the women lived in the hotel any longer, and having their own places to live changed their lives a good deal. In time each of them married, had their own children and became scions of the community.

Yuma was changing during those first years of ranching for Ralph and Ross, and for Jonas in his operation of the Palace. More businesses were growing in Yuma, the farming businesses were providing a lot of work for all those wishing to work hard in the heat of the summer and fall. Many people from northern Mexico, dissatisfied with the revolutionary times of the late 1800'smoved across the porous border into the U.S., began to learn the English language and establish their own businesses and farms in the area.

There was less gunplay on the streets, there were less ranchers growing only cattle for sale and transport to the east. There were less men spending most of their lonely days in saloons in the city and obtaining the only female companionship they were likely ever to know from ladies of the night. Churches had sprung up aside from the Methodist and Catholic churches. There were far more residents such as Janie and her parents than had been the case in all its previous history. Even so there were still people such as Robert Miller to contend with.

Manny, as a young teenager, needed to be in school according to the feelings of Ross and Flora so he stayed with Jonas, living in a room in the hotel, eating in the restaurant which the two of them put together within a year after Ross and Flora left. Manny learned well from Jonas and by the time he graduated high school and was awaiting marriage, he and Jonas had made the Palace into an even more profitable business. Those were the circumstances into which Robert Miller inserted himself when he tried to whup Manny.

When Jonas returned to the saloon and learned what had happened there on a Saturday afternoon he first sat down and laughed a lot. He said to Jake the barman, "You know I don't do this often Jake but pour me a cold one and a shot of the best we have. I have to celebrate this one." Manny walked in as Jonas was knocking back his shot of whiskey. Jonas was still laughing to himself.

Jonas said, "Come in here god- brother, let's have a drink together. I think you have earned it today and I damn sure feel good about what you did this afternoon." Jake poured another for each of them and Jonas and Manny sat down at a table where Manny explained what had happened earlier in the day. Jonas's only question about the entire thing was "Do you think the fool will try to come back at us again?"

"No," Manny said, but I do think we ought to talk to the sheriff about the entire thing. I would feel like a fool if the sheriff didn't know my father killed George Martin and your father killed William Martin. I also think maybe it would be wise to pay some attention to the threats he made against me and take some precautions for a time." Jonas sat quietly for a moment, tasting the whiskey as it rolled down the back of his throat and savoring the cool bitterness of the beer he used to chase the whiskey. He said "Manny all those days were so long ago I cannot believe this fool came here now to try and get revenge against our parents. The guy is either crazy or filled with hatred for everyone. I need to meet up with this guy." Jonas was shaking his head as he finished those words and then feeling the influence of the booze to a slight degree he said, "But not tonight my brother. Not tonight. We celebrate tonight the well-deserved ass kicking you administered to Robert Miller," and chuckled to himself again.

Manny was too full of the romance with his darling Janie to pay much attention to Robert Martin
and within a few minutes after his conversation with
Jonas he went off to see Janie. Their marriage was
scheduled for only a couple of weeks after the fight
with Martin. Manny didn't want anything to harm
them or their marriage plans. He left Jonas to see to
the early evening crowd which always was in the saloon on Saturday evenings.

It would not be a rowdy bunch but sometimes
someone would get a little too much "old loudmouth"
in himself and a fight would take place. Usually
Manny took care of those situations. Everyone in
town knew that he was tougher than nails in a fist
fight and that getting hit by him was like getting
kicked by a mule. Most often when he stepped into a
situation it ended then and there. Pretty much the
same was true of Jonas but for different reasons.
Manny was a nice young man despite being tough
as nails. Jonas was a full grown and very dangerous
man. Those who spent any time at all around the two
of them thought of Manny as a very nice young man,
and thought of Jonas as a bomb waiting to explode.

Jonas didn't just step into a situation involving
a fight, he finished both the fighters very quickly
in almost all cases with a punch or two, or with
his sap and then had them hauled off to jail. With

Manny, a fighter in the saloon got the crap beat out of him probably. With Jonas, it was a certainty and the fighter ended up in the jailhouse as well. People looked at Manny with some awe. Many looked at Jonas with some fear.

Jonas always carried a sap on his person while in the saloon. He would use it, he was known to use it and a few times he did use it. Because of those occasions the word got around that Jonas would not hesitate to put you to sleep. The word also got out that if he did sap you the next morning the sheriff would be telling you why you had to stay out of the jail and out of the saloon for a while.

Jonas thought the sap better than a bullet in the guts. But on those few occasions between 1895 and 1910 when it was necessary for him to strap on a pistol he had not hesitated for a moment to do just that. Jonas did not have the temperament that his father had. Jonas suffered idiots much better than did Ralph. He would not suffer someone out to get revenge against him and his family without knowing what seriousness existed in the mind of Robert Martin. For a few days after the fight in the Palace, Jonas searched the bars of Yuma for Martin.

He found Martin alone one afternoon in another saloon in Yuma. It was called the Cactus Bar, and it was one of those in which Robert's mother had worked as a prostitute. Jonas was known there as he was everywhere in the town of Yuma. He heard Martin was spending a lot of time there and without telling Manny he was going to confront Martin, Jonas went to the Cactus Bar. As he entered he spotted Martin right away standing next to the bar talking with the bartender. Jonas walked directly to Martin and standing to his side asked him, "Do you know who I am Mr. Martin?"

Martin answered, "Sure I know who you are, you are Jonas Forney. I know who you are for sure."

"Why are you here In Yuma, Mr. Martin?"

"Well Mr. Forney I thought you already knew the answer to your question. I am here to kill your friend Mr. Hendershot, and if you get in the way it will be my pleasure to send you on your way to hell as well." Martin had a smirk on his face which infuriated Jonas though no one could have known except for Jonas neck becoming a deep, dark red color.

"Apparently you are a slow learner Mr. Martin. Perhaps you would like a more violent repeat of the lesson Manny taught you the other day. Would you like another lesson of the same sort Mr. Martin?"

Martin made the mistake of puffing up as though he were prepared to fight Jonas. It was a total mismatch. Manny had speed and guile on his side when he punched Martin the first time. Jonas had strength, knowledge of how to fight and willingness unparalleled even by his younger god brother. If Manny's punch was like a mule kicking the recipient the punches landed by Jonas were even more punishing.

Jonas didn't wait for anything. He punched Martin in the gut on the right side as Martin began to turn toward him. The first punch bent Martin over slightly. Jonas hit Martin squarely on the temple with his second blow. Martin collapsed on the floor of the bar, out cold for the moment. Martin didn't move at all for a while, but Jonas did.

Jonas knew what would happen if he got close enough to the bartender. The bartender would whack him with a bung starter and knock him cold, then Jonas would get the beating of his life. But Jonas, knowing what would happen, did not allow it to occur. Once Martin was out cold he grabbed Martin by the hair and drug Martin out the front door of the bar leaving the bartender in the Cactus Bar standing there with a bung starter in his hands cussing Jonas roundly.

Outside, as Martin lay in the dirt of the street, Jonas waited patiently for Martin to reawaken. When Martin was fully awake Jonas began beating him again. Martin stood and made as if to throw a blow at Jonas, hitting only the air. He hit Martin three or four times in the ribcage area seeing Martin wince in pain with each of those blows, and then he hit Martin on the jaw and sat him down on the seat of his pants.

Once more he waited for Martin to wake up and stand up. As Martin stood, was fully erect and seemingly ready for the battle again Jonas began beating him again. The beatings began to become a series which went on for a quite some time. During the series of beatings he gave Martin several people saw what was occurring, after watching what was going on for a while, and with some after they applauded Jonas, and went to retrieve a deputy sheriff.

A deputy came along, stood and watched one of the series of beatings for a few minutes, then while Martin was sitting on the ground, shaking his head and trying to wake up, the deputy asked Jonas what was going on. Jonas told the deputy he was trying to persuade Martin to leave town. The deputy nodded, said "That'd be good," and left the two of them to their work. It continued for a time until Jonas grew tired of the one-sided nature of the fight. As Martin began to have some ability to understand, or at least seemed to, Jonas stopped beating him. Martin was aware enough to know that any attempt on his part to get at Jonas in the moment would end badly.

Martin stood quietly as Jonas said to him, "You are not welcome in this town Mr. Martin. Your father was not welcome here and neither are you. Ross Hendershot killed your father. If you are stupid enough to think you want revenge against him why don't you call him out when he and his wife come here for their son's wedding. He will be available, I guarantee it to be true, but frankly I doubt you have the balls to think about challenging a man who is willing to fight with a gun. I suggest to you very strongly you should leave Yuma and never, ever come back again."

Before leaving Martin, Jonas said to him, "If I ever see you again, on the streets of Yuma, or in a bar in which I am located, I will beat you in the same fashion as I have just beaten you. If ever I see you and you have a gun in your hand you will die within the next ten seconds. Do not doubt my words Mr. Martin, for I am deadly serious about this. Do you understand me clearly Martin?"

Martin mumbled something through his broken gums and teeth, and Jonas started to walk away. Jonas turned then, came back to Martin and said, "Disappear you piece of cow dung, and hit him one last blow to the jaw, leaving Martin unconscious. It seemed apparent Martin must have understood and taken Jason's suggestion for a time. No one saw him in or near the town of Yuma for several weeks. No one saw him because he went into California, to El Centro, some eighty miles or so away from Yuma and gotten himself a job as a drummer in a dry goods store in the little town of Brawley, near El Centro.

Martin went away but his mind was still occupied with trying to kill Ross Hendershot or maybe someone dear to Ross. Working in the dry goods store enabled him to buy an older pistol and ammunition for it. He took it to the desert and practiced with it as much as he could. Each practice session he set up a target which he labeled Manny and one he labeled Jonas as well. After the beating Martin absorbed from Jonas he intended to kill Jonas no matter what happened with the others.

4

Manny and Janie

June 1910

Manny and Janie were deeply in love with each other. Their ages, eighteen and seventeen respectively, enhanced their sense of fun in each other, made it possible for them to be both childishly playful and tease each other pleasantly and sexually constantly. Janie would not permit Manny to touch those places she would hold dear for him until their marriage. But she loved kissing him, and when he moaned he wanted her badly she would say, "You can wait. It's not much longer now. If I can wait you can wait my love." Then they would go back to teasing or kissing or simply walking together.

In a real way the two of them were very lucky to be growing up, to be in love, in the times in which they lived. There were no more restless and warring natives left in Arizona. The town in which they lived was well policed and had little impact from criminal conduct. They could walk in the countryside by the Colorado River without fear of encountering much of anything except rattlesnakes. In other words they were safe in their environment, something which had not always been true for young people in love in the Arizona Territory.

Human rattlesnakes were very rare in the Yuma of their times. Men whose lives depended on the use of the gun, and an inherent dishonesty toward society, were few and far between. Both Manny and Janie seemed to realize and appreciate the wonder of a peaceful place in which to grow up in love. Both took advantage of their freedom from fears which had been rife in the past in almost every community in the Arizona Territory.

Almost everyone who saw the two of them together smiled, thought of them as young and good looking and in love, and all those things were true. Their youth and the love so obvious which they held for each other was infectious to those around them.

Manny, sometimes a very private young man, was a little jealous of her contact with other men but mostly was protective of Janie in the extreme. He saddled her horse for her if they went riding, making sure, even though he understood she could accomplish the same task, the cinch was drawn tight so the saddle would not slip when she mounted. As they walked together he was constantly aware of wagons, horses being ridden around them, even the not so evident automobiles or motor driven cycles making their first appearances in Yuma.

He was also on the lookout for problems, and after he had beaten the bejesus out of Robert Martin he was aware of every other person around the two of them as well, but nothing happened. No one followed them or seemed to be trailing along with them in a parallel walk through the town. He saw no threats, no danger which was not always present under normal circumstances. Robert seemed to have gone away. They heard Robert was in El Centro or north of there. Manny relaxed his guard a little and so did Jonas. Neither thought Robert Martin to be a threat to them any longer.

As the time drew near for their wedding the two young people spent much more time with each other preparing themselves it seemed for the time when they would be together constantly. Then the long anticipated and hoped-for day arrived for their marriage. It was, Janie thought, a spectacularly pretty day, a spring moment of warmth but not heat, the sun shining brightly. As she dressed for her wedding, giggling with her mother and a group of her girlfriends, she thought the entire experience to be magical, magnificent, and seeing her husband to be waiting for her at the altar changed nothing in her outlook.

Manny looked wonderful in his dark suit but was very nervous just before the wedding began. Flora calmed him before hand, saying "You have gotten the best there is in this town Manny. You will be beautiful together. You will have beautiful children together. Be calm my son, let your love for her shine for all to see. One more thing my son, if you feel the urge to cry, do not be ashamed. You are, after all, my son and I know I will be crying my eyes out, in happiness for both of you."

Manny and Janie were married by the Methodist preacher both knew very well. His name was Malcolm Walker. Malcolm talked too long, taking advantage of a larger than normal and captive crowd in his church. He sermonized a little too much, but in the end it was a beautiful wedding. Malcolm was solemn, very serious as he administered the vows to them. His solemnity carried over to them, made them appear very serious about their vows, as they were.

Janie was lovely in a white flowing dress her mother had made from cloth ordered from New York City. It took the cloth nearly a year to arrive, but the wait was well worth it. Janie radiated beauty as she walked down the aisle to meet her husband. The wedding march was played on a brand new piano the Methodist church had purchased from San Francisco. It took months on end to arrive via steamer into the Gulf of California and "lighter" up the Colorado River to Yuma. Its sound was wonderful and the woman who played the wedding march gave a performance of her own which helped to solemnize the rites.

Manny's suit fit him wonderfully. His boots were new and had a high sheen that it had taken him a week to put on them. He wore no hat though many in the crowd, including his father and godfather, carried theirs into the church with them. His smile beamed. His words were so filled with the joy of the occasion that he had nothing but good to say to all. As Janie walked toward him he almost cried. Flora noted that a tear was rolling out of his eye and hers flowed more freely for her son's happiness. He kept thinking to himself as she walked toward him, God she is so beautiful, and she is mine forever. I am so lucky.

Ross was mesmerized by Janie's beauty. He and Ralph, along with Flora, Carmelita, Jason and his lady stopped at the Palace on their way to the wedding for a little liquid fortification. When he made his way to the room in which Manny was sequestered prior to the wedding his son made him promise not to drink too much in response to the event. One thing was greatly different for both Ralph and Ross, it being neither of them had any kind of weapon on them. Ross felt almost naked without a gun strapped to his side, but the occasion dictated no firearms and he was not only willing but happy to oblige.

Then, almost as if by magic the ceremony was over, the youngsters were newlyweds kissing in front of everyone as he whispered in her ear, "No holding back tonight my love."

Janie, the pert one, the sassy one, the wonderfully humorous one, peered into his eyes and said, "You better not drink too much today my lover for I am going to give you the ride of your very life today." And then she blushed a little and laughed out loud as they were almost skipping their way down the aisle. There were still conventions to be met, photographs to be taken, conversations to be held with parents and friends, toasts to be suffered, and the first dance of their lives together to enjoy for a whole variety of reasons.

A few moments were given over to pictures. Yuma though still a very small town even had a photographer by the time they married. Many townspeople bought copies of the wedding photographs simply out of its beauty. In time each of those who did so would stare at the photo of Manny and Janie and shake their head at the tragedy which followed months later.

Several moments after the ceremony were given over to hugs for parents and a moment of real love shared between Janie and Flora. A few moments were given over to the start of an ice cream social kind of thing and to the cutting of the cake in the church. Some prayers were offered and then all, including the preacher, left the church and went to the Palace for a party. At the Palace the party began with a shout from Ross, "The first round is on me."

His shout was followed in a few minutes by Jonas standing on the bar inviting everyone to "belly up" for another drink, this one on the house, while he said, "To my brother in all ways save by birth, and to his wonderful bride, congratulations to you both."

The first dance of marriage was shared between Janie and Manny, heads together, considering each other's eyes deeply, lovingly, the moments indelibly etching themselves into their memories. For the first time he felt the heat of her core below as she put herself very close to him indeed, and she in turn felt, for the first time directly against her core, the hardness and readiness of his manhood. It was almost an impossibility for her to break away from his arms when it came time to dance with others in the wedding party. For Manny those few moments of her dancing with Ross, Ralph, her own father, seemed interminable he wanted to hold her so badly.

She danced with Ralph, and with Ross, and with her father and brother, and even with the preacher among many others before coming back together with her husband. He danced with Carmelita and Flora, and Janie's mother, as well as many other women from the town, including Jonas' companion, Helen awaiting the time when his bride would return to him. As the dance was ending she came back to him, took him in her arms and danced with him for a moment before she led him off the floor to the cheers of the entire body of them all. The two of them retired to the same wonderful suite of rooms which Ross and Flora had shared so many years earlier. The suite was decorated differently, of course, and the canopy of the bed was draped with beautiful white muslin to keep them free of mosquitoes or gnats.

Their first night together as husband and wife was all she and Manny had thought it would be, had hoped it would be. She was a little shy as they undressed each other slowly, but gave in to her innate lustiness in short order. Finally they were both without clothing and it was time to explore. Their initial touches, born of wonder and love, were a bit halting, but rather quickly they both began to discover sensations each craved and the means to create those cravings with their hands, their lips, their very inner most desires being openly and unashamedly evident.

There was no urgency, nor any lack of care with each other. Both wished for a night long experience. They kissed, moved their kisses constantly, exploring places which had never been kissed before for first moments, then minutes. They touched, felt their bodies from tip to toe, knew each other in every part of their worldly being by the start to the end of the evening. She was far less experienced than he but his prior moments of lust had been brief and purposeful with a couple of ladies of the night.

This night was not for a quick anything. This night was for loving touching, for knowing, for making the moments of crescendo last as long as possible, then starting over to build to new, higher crescendos. His cries of joy were somewhat louder than hers as the evening started but as it lengthened that too changed. She laughed at him, and at herself, cried a little with the first flashing pain of his being inside her, let him dominate, then pushed him onto his back and took total control of him. Her initial shyness was not coquettish, but borne of inexperience.

Nearing midnight, she told him as they lay spent for the moment in their bed, "Go downstairs for a while. Dress lightly so they will know we have been busy. They will still be there, our parents, our friends. They are waiting for you to appear, you know. They will tease you a lot and leave an open question you must answer by simply telling them how much you love me and how much I love you. I will bathe quickly and come down to be with all of you in a few minutes. We will not stay there for long, my lover, my husband, we will soon be back in our wedding bed."

He dressed, complaining a little, saying "I want to bathe with you, to feel you on me, me in you, while we are surrounded by the warmth of the water. God, you are gorgeous woman. God, how I love you. I don't want to leave you. I don't want to ever leave you again, never my love." She came to him and held him, and pushed him toward the clothing laying on a chair where it had been hastily deposited earlier.

She laughed, loved on him for a minute and said, petting him briefly, "Go now my husband. I need some time to recover before I begin my ride to Phoenix. We only made it to Welton so far." She laughed as did he as she poked him on the nose joyfully and they separated for the moment.

Manny went to the saloon. He found his mother and father there, his godfather and Carmella there, a man he had never met named Manuel Esquerra and his lady, Jonas and his lady, the preacher who had consumed more beer than he probably should have and a lot of others including Janie's parents and siblings. They all shook his hand, clapped him on the back repeatedly, told him what a lucky young man he was and refrained from any comments about the time he and Janie had been missing.

Ross beamed with pride as he clapped his hands on his son's broad shoulders, a single tear tracing its way down his weather-beaten face. Flora wiped Ross's tear from his face and put it into her mouth. She exclaimed to all, it has been many years since I have seen a tear from these wonderful eyes and I wish it to remain with me, inside my being forever. I am so very proud of my two men tonight.

Ross brought Senor Esquerra to Manny and said to Manny, "This is one of my oldest friends, one of Ralph and my oldest friends I should say. This is a man on whom you can count no matter what, son. He should always be made welcome in this place. Jake knows what I say to be true and I think the rest of the barmen do as well, but I don't think you have met Senor Esquerra before."

Manny reached out his hand, Senor Esquerra took it, then pulled Manny to him and in the Mexican way greeted Manny with the abrazo, a hug and a pat on the back.

Manny had never experienced an abrazo before. He asked, "Senor is that the common way of greeting in Mexico?"

"Si Manuelo," Senor Esquerra said. "It is common among family and good friends. I have known your father and godfather for so long that I feel like I am family. Esta' bueno Senor Manuelo?"

"Si, Senor, usted es como mi tio. Gracias Senor. Despues de todo, tengo su nombre, verdad?" (Yes Senor, you are like my uncle. After all I have your name). Senor Esquerra smiled broadly and nodded his agreement and acceptance of Manny's statement and the three of them made their way to the bar. Ross called for the best of the house and it was served along with the standard cold beer chaser. It was a great moment of male bonding which was ended by the appearance of his bride. Senor Esquerra told Manny he wanted to toast the two of them when Janie made her appearance. She wore only a shirt draped over jeans and sandals but it was worn demurely.

As Janie came into the room several shots rang out from somewhere outside. They imbedded themselves into the wood of the building somewhere, making no threat to any of the revelers. Ross and Ralph looked outside but in moments the worry of more gunfire was forgotten. All thought it had been someone celebrating a little too much, someone who had taken in a little too much whiskey and fired off their gun into the sky in celebration.

After all the greetings had been renewed and all had their hands filled for toasts. Senor Esquerra offered an old Mexican toast Manny, among many others, loved. Janie slipped her arm around her husband, holding him close. Manuel said, "Por los dos de ustedes, por favor, por sus vidas como uno, Salud, Salud, y pesetas, y amor por sus vidas total, y el tiempo para gustarlos." (For the two of you, please, for your lives as one, health, wealth, and love for your entire life, and the time to enjoy them.)

All cheered, drank up and Manny and Janie sneaked away with only Flora noticing. When Ross asked what happened to them Flora just said for him to hush and think about their earliest days together. Nothing more needed to be said for Ross to understand. He smiled at Flora and nodded, thinking of their lust filled moments of coming together, the "Days of Flora," he had termed them. He leaned down to her ear and said "I love you my wife. Perhaps we should go off and do some of the same things our children are doing?"

She laughed, turned to him and kissed him for a long time and then said to all as she dragged him away from the table toward the hotel, "I think my man has some needs that we are both needed to fulfill. We will see you all tomorrow." Soon Ralph and Carmella did the same as did Jonas and his amour named Helen. Jake, the manager of the saloon for the night, closed the place down after the rest of the crowd slowly dispersed and went home to his family. He and his wife enjoyed a happy discussion of all the events of the day and followed the pathway set by Manny and the rest in short order.

Ralph and Carmelita, Ross and Flora stayed on in the hotel after the wedding for several days, as did Manuel Esquerra and his wife. Within a week the three couples returned to their ranches in Mexico, leaving Manny and Jonas to manage the hotel once again. Normalcy returned to the town, adding one young couple to its population. The hotel, restaurant and bar continued to thrive. Neither Jonas or Manny saw anything of Robert Martin in the weeks following the wedding. Both became unconcerned about Robert coming back to cause them any kind of problem.

During the next several weeks Manny and Janie became a regular item in town, when they took a break from working or the bedroom, strolling on the wooden sidewalks, Manny doffing his hat to the ladies of the town, Janie giving a mock curtsy to the gentlemen of the town as they passed by each. Oft times they would stop and converse with another couple also out for a stroll.

Few of the couples in the small, but growing town, were as young as Manny and Janie, but all were infatuated with them. It was only natural for friendships to form, common courtesies to be observed, especially in Janie's eyes. She saw part of the conventions of being married as involving the willingness to befriend other couples in the community.

The two of them attended church regularly and were greeted there enthusiastically by all. Janie's parents were very involved in the operation of the church and were terribly pleased the young couple was willing to attend regularly. Manny was not a terribly religious man and carped a little about the necessity of going every Sunday. It was the one demand Janie made of Manny and while carping a little he knew it was something she wanted and therefore was willing to accept her request.

They were a part of the town, young, in love, happy to be there and with each other, and it was amazing how their good humor seemed to spread in the town. When they went out she always insisted on wearing a nice dress and insisted that he wear a suit. They were a very handsome couple together who had become one in a short time and she wanted the world to be aware of their relationship.

Their smiles were infectious. They caused others to smile at them and at each other. Couples took note of the loving nature of the way the two of them walked, sometimes brushing against each other, sometimes holding hands, sometimes being arm in arm and close together. The entire town seemed to love them, to look forward to seeing them together and on the streets of the dusty western town. Their loving ways became an infection amongst the rest of the married couples in town. Smiles broke out on a lot of faces. Loving touches by other couples were much more commonplace than prior to their marriage. Even a stolen kiss, sometimes more passionate than at others, was seen to take place on the streets of Yuma with other couples.

Many in the town remarked what a beautiful young couple they were and how pretty their children would be. Manny and Janie remarked to each other from time to time it was so wonderful to be alive, and so much in love, and to be loved in their town as well. It was obvious even to them the town revered them both, and their love for each other made their natural lust for each other even more consuming. She grew to enjoy and crave their love making even more than him.

Many times indeed it was she initiated their dance of love, first with a little brush against him, a well-placed moment of contact between his arm and her breast, or maybe just a teasing comment. Whatever the means of initiation they were in and out of bed often every day. All who worked in the hotel simply smiled as they saw Manny and Janie climbing the stairs to their suite two or three and sometimes many more times a day. No one doubted their purpose or intent when they disappeared from the bar or hotel area.

About three months after their marriage as they sat in the restaurant/saloon eating their dinner Janie said to Manny, "Are you ready to take on the role of being a father my husband?" As his jaw dropped and he was stunned by her question she said, "Of course you are. You are one of the best men I have ever known in my entire life. If you were not I would not have married you."

He looked at her, stared into her eyes, his eyes brimming with tears as she had known they would, took her hand in his, kissed her hand, and said, "Oh my God Janie are you sure? Are you sure my love?"

"Well I am as sure as a girl can be Manny Hendershot. I have talked a lot with my mother about the signs and symptoms of being pregnant and I think in about seven or eight months we are going to have a little one my darling." They nattered on for hours about whether the child would be a boy or a girl, finally deciding it would make no difference to either of them which gender it was, so long as the baby was healthy.

They talked for the first time about getting a place of their own, outside the hotel. The suite in which they lived was wonderful but it was not a home, not a place she could make into their nest both for them and for their children. The conversations about the baby began to be a daily occurrence with Jonas and Helen taking part, with others in town, when they were told the good news being thrilled for Manny and Janie.

It was a wonderful day for the two of them, the first moments of both knowing, but for one thing which was Ross and Flora and indeed Ralph and Carmella were not there to share their happiness. Both knew Flora and Carmella would come later to help Janie along with her mother. Janie wrote a letter to each of them so Flora and Carmella would know she was pregnant. It took a while for the two letters to come to their destinations but both Flora and Carmella were ecstatic and each began to plan for going to Yuma for the birthing.

Flora began to think about how she could go to Yuma to be of help to Janie. Flora, many years earlier, had asked Manuel Esquerra to come and work with her and Ross at the ranch. It would be easy for her and Ross to go to Yuma and leave the operation of the ranch to Manuel. If Manuel wanted to come along, and he probably would, there were trusted men amongst the few campesinos they had working there who loved Manuel. Manuel knew everything he needed to know to make the ranch run smoothly during her and Ross's absence and if he chose to come he could impart the needs of the ranch to men who would take care of everything. Then horror struck them all. Within days of the letter telling of Janie's pregnancy arriving the news of Janie's passing also arrived.

Flora was devastated, Ross was in shock. Carmelita began to put together food for Ralph right away, as did Flora for Ross. No words were spoken of the need to go to Yuma. Flora would follow as soon as she felt comfortable, but within a matter of days. Carmelita was already on her way when Flora left the ranch. Ross began to put his kit together for the ride to Yuma within hours after the arrival of the news. He and Flora talked and it was agreed that he and Ralph would go first, Flora and Carmelita would follow when Ross sent word he and Ralph had arrived in Yuma. Manuel would stay and run the ranch or if he wished he would come with Flora. As Ross began to put together his saddle guns and his holsters and pistols Flora asked him, "Don't you think you are getting a little old for this kind of trail riding my love?"

Ross's laconic reply was sufficient to end further commentary on the subject. He answered, "Manny needs our help, darling. Jonas will be trying to find out where the killer is and as soon as we arrive we will most likely be heading out again." She nodded and he continued working to get him ready for the trip. It was only a few hours after the telegram arrived at the ranch when Ross left.

5

Oh Janie, Oh Janie Where Have You Gone?

October 1910

Manny and his bride Janie continued their work in
the Palace with Jonas daily. They also decided to take
a "constitutional" walk every day since they knew
she was pregnant. Not many babies had been born in
the new Yuma Hospital. It was not large and didn't
have a lot of rooms for people to stay but it did have

a good doctor who had trained some back in the east in the delivery of children.

The doctor also had the good sense to know mid-wives were useful in the process and planned on having a mid-wife in attendance when it came time for Janie to deliver her baby. Janie thought it should be Flora and Carmelita, both women having helped others to deliver children in their past. The Doctor raised no objections to either or both women being there. He had known both for many years.

Janie began to show signs of her pregnancy within two months and by three months it was evident to anyone she was with child. Everyone in town was excited for the event of the birth of Manny and Janie's child. Women would stop her on the street and ask her when she thought the baby would come and give her advice as to how to eat and live her life prior to the baby being born. It was fun for her, even fun for Manny when those discussions took place. One of the comments which was made as a rule was "I bet your baby will be as beautiful as you are Janie." People would ask if she wanted a boy or girl. She would say in response all she wanted was a healthy baby.

One windy Yuma day when there was a lot of dust in the air, she and Manny set off for their usual walk. Despite the wind and the dust they thought she needed the exercise so off they went. There were few people on the streets. It was one of those desert days when no one wanted to be out and about unless it was a necessity.

As it turned out, when they got outside and experienced the ugliness of the weather where it was blowing too hard, there was too much dust, right away she was uncomfortable about being out in the weather and Manny realized it. After they got about a block and a half away from the Palace where the two of them resided they decided to turn around and go back to the hotel. The wind and the dust were just too much for them and they thought probably it was not good for the baby as well. It was a little difficult to see, the air was full of sand, it just was not a day to be outside. They never made it home.

Robert Martin arrived back in town the day prior to this fateful walk by the Hendershot youngsters. He had not gone by the sheriff's office yet because he did not want to give up his gun. It was hidden under his duster and coat as he went to another bar besides the Palace and had a few shots of whiskey to brace himself. He fully intended to go to the Palace and kill both Manny and Jonas. He needed the fortification to do the deed. He meant to finish the task the very same day. Some, in the bar where Martin fortified himself, wondered what the hell he was doing back in town.

No one there really thought much of him but they didn't bother him either.

Martin staggered out of the bar intending to get on his horse and find a livery in which he could house the horse and go to sleep. Before walking out of the bar he pulled his bandanna up over his mouth and nose to keep out the sand. As he left the bar he saw the back of Manny and his wife scurrying out of the dust storm. Martin's horse was closer to the Hendershots than it was to Martin and he headed in the direction of the horse. As he stumbled along he recognized Manny and Janie, drew his gun and headed in their direction.

Robert began to walk and then run toward Manny and Janie screaming Manny's name as he ran. Manny never saw Robert until the shots rang out. Robert pulled his pistol out of his clothing as he ran, and when he was around fifty yards away from them, being drunk enough he could not properly estimate distances, he began to shoot in their direction. He emptied his pistol even though he didn't realize he had done so. He was nearly as bad a shot as his father had been. One of the bullets hit Manny and another hit Janie.

Robert passed by the sheriff's office as he was running and he was maybe fifty feet past it when he started shooting at Manny and Janie. Both went down as he fired. Martin continued toward them but heard a gunshot from behind him. He turned partially and saw the sheriff leveling a pistol at him. Martin broke his forward stride toward the Hendershots and ran down an alley, gathering his horse in the process. As the sheriff arrived at the alley he saw Martin riding away into the dust. Martin was already too far away for accurate pistol fire. The sheriff went directly to Manny and Janie.

The sheriff knew who was down and why. He ran to Manny and saw Manny had received a flesh wound alongside and under his arm. He checked Janie and saw where a bullet had hit her squarely in the middle of the back of her dress. He put a hand in front of her mouth and felt no breath. Her body was limp, she was not breathing, she was already gone and the sheriff knew it. He started to say something to Manny, to get him to lay Janie down so the extent of Manny's wound could be determined.

Manny was holding Janie tightly to him and talking to her, telling her "I love you honey. You are going to be all right. Hang on, honey. The doctor will be here soon. I love you, honey." Manny repeated himself over and over again, rocking Janie in his arms. When the doctor came and saw the situation he gave Manny a glass of what appeared to be booze. It was laudanum and it put Manny to sleep. It was the only way he could retrieve Janie's dead body from Manny's arms.

After Manny was asleep the doctor, with the help of one of the local ladies, took Janie into his office and cut the back of her dress. He looked at the bullet hole and saw that it was almost dead center. He cut the front of her dress to see if it was a through and through, but it was not. There was a growing bruise on the center of her chest between her callow breasts and there was no heartbeat or respirations. Janie was gone. She had been gone from the instant she was shot for all practical purposes.

The doctor, knowing Manny would be beside himself with agony over his wife's untimely death, took Manny to the hospital. He sent the sheriff to tell Jonas what had happened. He sent another man to tell Janie's parents what had happened. Jake was alone in the saloon, and Jonas was in San Luis. A man who worked in the saloon from time to time as a swamper was sent to San Luis to notify Jonas. Janie's parents, devastated, crying, took their daughter's body home with them to prepare her body for the undertaker. Janie's mother cleaned all the blood from Janie, dressed her demurely in underclothing and called for the undertaker to come. She would be buried two days later. Manny was kept under the laudanum on

Jonas' orders to the doctor for several days after the burial.

The doctor kept giving Manny doses of laudanum for the day after the shooting even while a posse searched for Robert. The posse, under the leadership of Sheriff Josiah Hamilton, left town right away looking for Robert Martin, but they found nothing. Jonas had been in San Luis when this all happened. No one knew where he was but for Jake and Jake thought it best to let Jonas decide about whether Manny should be brought out from under the drug. Jonas thought it best Manny have at least a day to heal from his own gunshot wound, before the burial. Then he could be brought out and told of Janie's death.

Learning of Janie's death would be the hardest moment of Manny's short life, and Jonas meant to be the one who told Manny about her passing. Jonas saw to it Janie was placed in a silk lined casket, dressed in the finest linen for her eternal sleep. He was told by the undertaker her body would begin to go sour in a way which could not be covered in about two days. The funeral was set for three days after her death.

By the time the posse was back a day later, Jonas was home and Manny, cleaned up, sewed up where the bullet had grooved the skin of his ribs, and constantly half drunk at least, was home at the Palace. Manny was inconsolable, sobbing in spasms of grief over and over throughout the day. It had been the most difficult task of Jonas life to tell Manny of Janie's death. Jonas could find no words adequate to voice his sorrow for them all but particularly for his brother. Jonas tried very hard to help Manny but it was impossible for him to understand why his bride was gone. Manny stayed mostly drunk up until the day of the funeral.

The funeral was held in the Methodist Church which gave way to a crowd so large that it spilled out into the street. The preacher was loquacious and persuasive Janie would meet them all in heaven. He was convinced she was such a sweet and pure heart she probably was already there. Jonas and Jonas' lady, Helen sat in the front row with Janie's parents. Manny sat between Jonas and Helen, crying through the entire service. He asked Jonas to see Janie prior to the funeral. She looked beautiful in her white linen even though her skin had begun to mottle with the decomposition of her body.

Manny cried throughout the ceremony and after everyone was headed for the burial he nearly fell to pieces in his god-brother's arms as he keened and screamed out his lament, "Oh Janie, oh Janie, where are you my love?" Then, stumbling with the pain of walking he was guided by Jonas and Jake to the buggy in which the three of them rode to the cemetery. He continued his keening at the cemetery.

Jonas, the strong one, the quiet one, the angry one in those moments, angry at the murder of his little "sister," cried quietly himself, his tears meandering down his cheeks with no shame and no attempt at concealment. Helen helped him clean his face and provided him with a handkerchief so he could blow his nose as the graveside services finished. As Jonas dropped handfuls of dirt onto the casket for himself he vowed he would find the son of a bitch who had done this terrible deed, find him and then, well the decision of what to do then would have to abide the time when they had Robert Martin under their control.

The undertaker had done a wonderful job for Janie. He had dressed her all in white and laid her into a white, lustrous material satiny in appearance if not in truth, in a coffin made of the finest wood he had available. One end of the coffin remained open at Manny's request. Manny wanted one last opportunity to see her and kiss her sweet face before he put her into the ground forever. Manny had asked the undertaker to take extra good care of his beloved. The undertaker wanted to make sure it appeared she was comfortable in her repose. He accomplished his task.

Her little head was cushioned and she looked peaceful and asleep as much as anything. The make-up he had used was beginning to fail as she was laid to rest. Her body was changing and the time had come to put her in the ground. The people filed by her casket one by one, throwing flowers on the end which was not open. When all were gone save for Manny, Jonas and Helen, it was time for Jonas and then Manny to pay their last moments of respect to Janie.

After Manny put his wedding ring onto his bride's finger to wed himself to her for all eternity the under-taker closed the casket and she was laid into the sod from which she came. Manny and Jonas remained to put the first deposits of earth on her final resting place. Both cried through it all, both had loved her though Manny much more so than Jonas. A few people, including the sheriff and the preacher stayed behind at the gates of the cemetery to wish Jonas and Manny well as they left to go back to the Palace.

At the Palace they would await the arrival of their parents. Manny held no anger at the cemetery but he did, in a fashion the same as his brother, vow to catch Robert Martin, and like Jonas he too had to set aside what would be done to Martin. He could not think about that part of the entirety of it all on the day of the burial.

Manny, Jonas and Helen rode back to the Palace with the undertaker on the beautiful black hearse which was pulled by two steeds, both black in color, and both clean and shined for this day. Jonas went behind the bar and took out a bottle of the best whiskey they had. He meant to get his brother good and drunk so Manny would sleep for the night at least. It was a task he didn't think would be too difficult to accomplish given the emotional state Manny was in when they returned to the hotel.

The sheriff came in as the two of them sat with Jake and Helen alone in the saloon in the early afternoon. He told Jonas as they stood together at the bar no one had heard anything about where Martin might have gone. Jonas thought there might be someone in the Cactus Bar who would have a little information. Jonas told the sheriff he was going to carry a pistol when he went to the Cactus Bar later to try and pry some information from anyone who might have it.

The sheriff only nodded and said, "If you shoot anyone make sure they have a weapon of some kind on them. Jonas understood, but he could not and would not leave until he saw to it that his brother was asleep. Within an hour or so after coming from the cemetery Manny's head was bobbing up and down from the emotional drain of the times and the effects of the alcohol. Jonas put him to bed, said to Helen he had to go out for a little while, put a pistol in a small holster at the back of his pants covered by his frock coat, and went to the saloon one more time.

Jonas went to the saloon to tell Jake what he was going to do and where he was going. He wanted Jake to know all those facts in case somehow he disappeared forever. Jake almost laughed when Jonas said why he was telling Jake about his intended visit to the Cactus Bar, but understood Jonas' desire to make sure someone would guide Ross and Ralph to the right starting place if need be. Jake didn't think Jonas would have any trouble. He had the blood in his eye and no one would want to cross his path in this night in a negative way.

Jonas entered the Cactus Bar as the gloom of the evening began to fall over the town. The gloom was emphasized and enhanced by the necessities of the day, the necessity being laying sweet Janie to rest. There were many in the Cactus Bar when he got there. Some of the regulars from the Palace were there as well as the usual crowd which gathered regularly in the Cactus Bar. They had wanted to drink, to mourn Janie in their own way, but they had not wanted to disturb Jonas, Manny and the others in the Palace. Right away as he entered the bar those men and a few women came to him, some hugged him, some shook his hand, some just stopped, said "I'm sorry," and went on their way. Soon the room was much less filled with people than it had been.

Jonas stood at the end of the bar where he had felled Martin. He stood back away from the bar so the barman could not slug him with a bung starter. The barman came to him, sidled up to the bar and said, "You need not be fearful I will do anything to help the son-of-a-bitch here tonight Jonas. I have put my bung starter on the bar here next to you so you will know for sure I am telling you the truth. Now what can I get you?"

Jonas shrugged, looked at the man and said, "Do you have a good whiskey you personally drink?"

"Certainly. Would you like some of my stock?"

"Yes, and a beer as well please."

"I'm afraid our beer is not cold here like it is at your place Jonas," the barman said.

"It's all right man, I have had a lot of warm beer in my lifetime, and some of it is a lot better than the cold quite frankly." There were several men seated at a table in a corner of the bar who had been talking amongst themselves since Jonas came in the door. He overheard one of them say, "Go on Henry, you go on and talk to the man." Jonas stepped further sideways then and slowly put his hand behind him to draw his gun if it became a necessity.

The barman busied himself getting Jonas a drink, a bottle from which he could pour another if he chose and a glass of warm beer. As the barman was doing those things the man who had been called Henry by a friend walked over and stood within a foot or two of Jonas. As Henry came closer he raised his hands above his waist and said to Jonas quietly, "I am not armed Mr. Forney. Yes, I know who you are. I am not armed and I did not come to you to create trouble. I would like to talk with you."

Jonas had watched the man carefully. He took his hand out from behind him and said, "Then let's talk, sir." Jonas hoped this would be the moment when he would get information which would help he, Manny, Ralph and Ross to find and capture Martin. He waited.

The man nodded toward the bottle. Jonas nodded in return and the man poured himself a drink. Then he said, "Mr. Forney, Robert Martin is my friend. I have known him since he was a little boy. I know Ross Hendershot killed his father, but I also know his father was not worth much. The same applies to William Martin who I believe your father shot down in the street by the smithy's shop. Everyone in Yuma knew George Martin and William Martin were not worth a tinker's damn. I would not bother you, and I tell you for a fact there is not one man in this place who would bother you for a moment if you took a gun out and shot Robert Martin right in front of us all." Jonas just looked at the man, said nothing in return.

"So, Jonas Forney, I have been designated by all of us who are friends with Robert Martin to tell you he is headed for El Centro and probably beyond to the little town of Calipatria. He has a woman he stays with who works as a prostitute in the mining areas to the northwest of El Centro. Most likely Robert will be in a tiny little town to the north and east of El Centro called Calipatria. I hope the information is helpful to you and your family sir. We, all of us here tonight, all of us who I have talked with feel the same about Robert and what he did."

"What is your name please, sir?" Jonas asked.

"Henry. I am Henry Fellows." Henry was still a little hesitant in his attitude toward Jonas, but he appreciated the attention Jonas gave him. He waited to see what would follow.

Jonas extended his hand to Henry and shook his hand vigorously. He said to Henry as he did, "You are a man sir. My family is in change right now. We will be deciding as the events require it, as to how to handle Mr. Martin and his murderous attack on my brother and his wife in time. I take my hat off to you now. You have given me something to consider for sure, not just where Martin is sir, but his situation. I applaud you and invite you to come to the Palace and enjoy our hospitality. Please know you will be welcome any time in the Palace. Though you and your friends could have chosen sides with Martin you have remained neutral and yet have exhibited the best a man can show, courage and sound judgment. You and your friends," Jonas smiled wryly and said, "except for Mr. Martin himself, will be welcome in the Palace. For you Mr. Fellows your first drink and cold beer will be at my expense. Please come by and see us as you are able sir."

The barman came with Jonas' drink and a glass of beer for each of them. He poured one for Henry and himself as well. He raised his glass to Henry and said "Congratulations Henry. You have done a good thing here tonight, and to you Mr. Forney. We are all taken aback by the actions of Robert Martin. None of us would have ever seen anything bad happen to Manny's lovely young lady if given a choice in the matter, please believe me." He shook his head, lowered his gaze for a moment. "She was a beautiful young girl. I attend the Methodist church myself and I have seen here there many times. What Robert did is simply beyond anything except for me to say he was wrong."

The sheriff stepped in the door just then. He thought he had given Jonas enough time to create havoc, or not. He didn't know what he might be seeing when he came in. He almost expected to see more than one man on the floor bleeding. He had given Jonas an hour within which to attempt to get information about Robert. As he opened the door he had his hand on his gun. He looked in and saw Jonas at the bar with the barman and Henry Fellows and walked over and joined them. The three were smiling at each other and sharing a drink. He asked, "How all you men doing?"

Camaraderie between enemies is an amazing thing. In due time and with enough "oil" in their systems each of these men went away from this fateful conclave full of moments of friendship. Amazingly if Henry and Jonas had encountered each other in the same setting again within a matter of days earlier they probably would have come to blows with each other. Murder most foul has a way of changing perceptions though, and the perception of Robert Martin held by Henry and his friends had been altered to be sure.

On this occasion these former adversaries drank, clapped each other on the back, gave compliments to each other, acted like long lost best friends. All of them left this encounter well oiled, more than just a little inebriated. The next morning each of them had a massive headache, a sick feeling in their stomachs and an unwillingness to face the world. All of them also awoke with some satisfaction they had been able to communicate without fisticuffs, without the use of a weapon. Jonas, because his brother was in such deep mourning, had to arise, had to see to it Manny did not choose to wander off somewhere with a gun and end it all and he had to see to the operation of the business.

When Jonas arose and found Manny in the saloon he announced, "I know where Robert Martin is."

Manny, the impatient one responded, "Let's go, let's get saddled up and out of here. Where is the son-of-a-whore? Come on brother, let's get this job done so I can die in peace." Manny's statement confirmed for Jonas his worst thoughts, his worst realizations. He felt strongly Manny was leaning toward suicide. Manny's words made it a certainty in Jonas' mind.

Jonas poured another drink to give to Manny who was already feeling no pain at all and kept Manny drinking for a short while until Manny decided he needed to go back to sleep. Manny had forgotten all about Robert Martin as he stood at the end of the bar in the Palace and leaked tears for his love, drowning his remorse and grief. Jake and Jonas managed to get him to a hotel room for some much-needed sleep. After they put him to bed Jake asked, "Were you serious Jonas. Did you really find out where Martin is?"

"Yes, for sure, but doing anything about it for now has to await the arrival of our fathers. We don't know what kind of situation we might encounter if we head out to chase him down. We will try to get a little more information before we take those steps." Jake noticed Jonas did not tell him where Martin was located but Jake did not pry. He knew Jonas would let him know when the time was right.

Jonas had no intention of going anywhere to chase after Robert Martin, even though he knew he could do the job by himself if need be, until his father and godfather arrived. The telegram from Nogales telling him Ross and Ralph were on the way had come the prior day. He would wait now, wait for older, more experienced counsel, for the wisdom and years of Ross and Ralph. He would wait for them to come and then he and Manny would ride with them to find Robert Martin. When they did, well who knew what would happen? He decided to see if the sheriff knew anything about Calipatria and whether it had any law enforcement at all. What might happen in the "chase" might be heavily influenced by a little more information.

6

The Ride to Yuma Concludes

Early November 1910

As Ross and Ralph rode into San Luis Potosi', Sonora
the Alcalde (Mayor) of the town came out of his of-
fices to meet them in the center of the main street.
Everyone in the community had heard of their ride
to Yuma and the sad reason for the ride. The people of the town gathered around the mayor awaiting
Ross and Ralph. They were quiet, murmurs passed
through the crowd but there were no loud voices
heard. Though neither Ross nor Ralph was in San

106

Luis often they were both known there for their own exploits and for their wives who both came from the area. The gathering of the people was a showing of respect for the men, for their family, and for their grief.

The Alcalde, or Mayor, greeted them both warmly as they dismounted and walked to him with the "abrazo" and told them how sad it was that they were traveling to Yuma because of the death of Janie. In his time as Alcalde he had traveled to Yuma and had stayed at the palace. In doing so he had made acquaintance with both Manny and Janie. He said that despite the reason for their travel he was happy to see them and invited them into his home. As they began to gather their horses and possibles, the crowd patted them on the shoulders and murmured its sadness at Janie's death. The Alcalde's name was Estevan Casillas de Morago. His wife's name was Bonita. She greeted them warmly in Spanish and English as well and invited them to sit down and have something to drink to cool them from their long, hot ride.

Ross responded he would love some tea or just water but he must first see to his horse before he did anything else. Ralph concurred. The Alcalde said, "Es de no momento Senores, no le hace," (it is of no moment men), "ellos esta' bueno. Mis amigos, the people of my city are seeing to the needs of your horses right now. We could do nothing less, que no?" Mrs. Casillas brought them water and some small items of food along with tall glasses of beer and a shot of tequila each. The Alcalde ceremoniously led them in a drink to the health of their sons Manny and Jonas and politely asked as to the health and welfare of their wives.

Ralph answered Carmelita was fine and would soon leave the ranch with the foreman in control while they were both away to come to Yuma as well. He said she should pass through San Luis within several days. Ross indicated the same about Flora. Ross asked, "Is there any word at all concerning the man we will seek being in Mexico Senor Casillas?" This would be a ticklish topic if indeed Martin had been caught or was known to be in Mexico. The difference between the laws of Mexico and the U.S. would mean negotiations and perhaps even payment to enable Martin to be removed from Mexico.

Senor Cassillas had no information about Martin though. He said, "No Senor Ross. In fact, we have made it clear across the face of the border he is not welcome in our country. No one would do anything to hurt him badly, mind you, but he would be quietly sent back to wherever he was coming from if he tried to enter Mexico." Ross noted well the mention of the authorities not hurting Martin badly if he was found in Mexico. Senor Casillas went on to tell Ross and Ralph a general description of the man had been circulated to the west to Calexico, south of El Centro, California. He also said that rumors out of Yuma indicated that the man, Martin, was in or around Calipatria, California, slightly to the north and west of El Centro. It was said, the Alcalde told them, he was living in the small town with a woman who was supporting him.

Senor Casillas entered the discussion of Janie's death hesitantly by saying, "Senores I do not know if you wish to discuss the reasons for your travel with me, other than as to Senor Martin. I want to tell you my wife and I traveled to Yuma and met both Manny and Janie last year. They were both most gracious to us as was Jonas who put us up in a wonderful suite of rooms at the Palace. We fully expected to pay for those services which we received in the hotel, restaurante and saloon but Senor Forney would not hear of it. His hospitality and graciousness, along with Manny and Janie was beyond our wildest expectations. We are most assuredly very sorry for the loss of this wonderful young woman." Ralph could hardly keep from leaking tears as Senor Casillas talked and Ross's reaction was great sadness. It was clear to Senor Casillas it was not necessary to say more about the topic until later, perhaps.

Ross asked if there was a hotel nearby where they could clean up and rest for the night before continuing to Yuma. The Alcalde said, "No, no sir. But my humble home is yours for this night sir. In fact my wife is, I believe, drawing water for your bathing now." After the three of them finished the snacks provided by Mrs. Casillas the Senor took them to separate rooms in the back of the hacienda where baths with water steaming were already prepared and said, "When you have disrobed please hang your clothes on the chair outside the door and they will be tended to while you bathe."

Ross tried to say thank you, as did Ralph, but they were quieted by the comment from Senor Casillas he was only doing what Ross or Ralph himself would do in reverse circumstances. It was enough for the moment which led them into the steaming waters quickly.

Both Ross and Ralph fell asleep in the warm water of the tubs in which they bathed. Both had unseen young women who came in from time to time and added hot water to the tub as they slept. Both had been extremely tired without realizing just how tired they were. Both awakened with a start in time, finished their washing up and got out of the tubs. They found their clothes dusted and cleaned with the wrinkles a little less noticeable when they dressed. Both slept in the bed nearby to the tub after their bath as had been intended by the Senor.

The next morning, fully dressed and ready again for the trail, they found Senor Casillas and his wife waiting for them in the kitchen and dining area to which they were directed by the household servants. The Casillas would not hear of the two men leaving without a meal. After eating a wonderful and hearty breakfast and taking their leave, they were once again ready to hit the trail. Senor Casillas and his wife walked with then to their horses and saluted them as they prepared to leave.

As they mounted their horses Senor Casillas gently reminded them of their reason for traveling, without meaning to do so, when he said, "Please convey to Senor Manny my deepest sympathies, and those of my wife. We were privileged to have met his young lady a few months prior to their wedding. She was not only a beautiful girl but she was, as we say, muy simpatico as well. I am certain these times will be tremendously difficult for him as they would for any caring man. His love for his wife was evident well before they were married. It will be a difficult moment for all of you when you arrive in Yuma. If there is anything at all we can do to help please do not hesitate to ask Senores." The men were directed to follow a young rider who would accompany them to the border area and put them on the right path to connect with the Colorado River.

It was only a few miles to the border where they crossed into the U.S. and a few miles further to arrive at the banks of the Colorado River which they would follow into Yuma. The young caballero who accompanied them said little on the ride, let Ralph, Ross and their horses dictate the pace, and peeled off with an "Adios Amigos," as they saw the river in the distance. Their trek would end in a day or two. There was every likelihood another trek would follow according to the information Senor Casillas had provided. The decisions which would then be necessary would abide the time passing. They mentioned these things in desultory conversations as the horses wended their way along the banks of the river, without resolving anything.

It would be about a full two-day ride for them to get to Yuma. Late in the afternoon, after pushing the horses a little, they found a good place to camp, hobbled the horses so they could browse the area around them, gave the horses water and some grain and set about getting a fire going for cooking the rabbits they had taken along the way to eat for dinner. They put the rabbit meat on spits and cooked it next to a very hot fire of coals which burned down from the mesquite and Palo Verde wood which was in abundance on the ground. The meat was fine. They supplemented the meat with a kind of gruel made of ground corn and a little water. The fire would be allowed to go down during the night but the next morning would heat coffee before they left near dawn.

There were no incidents during the evening. They expected none and were not surprised when no rustlers or posse members, or wild natives came at them out of the brush alongside the river. The country was mostly pacified by 1910. The natives almost never caused any kind of problems for anyone. There were a few "highwaymen" left along the roads and byways of the country but very few. There were a few "rustlers" left but mostly in other areas of the territory of Arizona. Most of the cattle ranches were gone from the Yuma area. Irrigated farm lands had replaced the ranging cattle and exotic crops abounded. The ride into the area of Yuma during the day would be peaceful and reflective.

As they rode Ross thought back to the times of their pasts in Yuma. Ralph did the same. Those times were painful in some respects for Ralph and his brow knit some as they rode and he remembered the times when his wife Georgi and his daughter Jenny had died near the town. But he also had the fond memory of having met his beloved Carmelita while he, Ross and Flora were running the Palace Hotel, Saloon and Fancy House.

For a moment Ralph thought to himself, I wonder how badly the urge for revenge will eat at Manny. He is a good man and I cannot believe he will let it consume him as it nearly did me. I'm glad Ross was there to talk some sense to me and help me face the fact that I couldn't take the law in my own hands. It is good Ross will be here, along with Manny and Jonas, to help us all escape the urge to draw and quarter Martin. He said to Ross, "Do you remember talking to me like a Dutch uncle on our first ride up to La Paz and back?"

"Well, yeah but I would have to admit the memory is a little dim," Ross replied.

"I'm not saying it will be necessary, I know what a good young man Manny is and he may not have any desire for revenge. It is likely those feelings will be strong though Ross. Just thought I would remind you how you persuaded me I should let the law take its course with the piece of shit who murdered my Jenny. You know I wanted to gut Jason Grant. I don't think I ever said thank you for bringing me back to earth. You may have to do the same with Manny."

"Well if it was me I would want to gut the son of a bitch Martin with a dull knife," Ross said. "You are probably right pard. I had forgotten how bad you wanted to kill Jason I guess. If I know my son he will be pretty well cranked up to do the same with Robert Martin I would guess, and not without reason, just as you were not without reason in your feelings Ralph."

"Even so pard you may have to stand in the way of your son killing Martin. It may come to it. I'll be right there with you of course. I would guess because of what happened to my Jenny I may have some pull with Manny, but he is your boy and you will have to be the one to stop him."

While Ross thought about what Ralph had to say he also thought about the times he had spent in Yuma, how they began their loving relationship, he and Flora, how those times were something for which he would be ever grateful. They had ended in one sense with the business he, Flora and Ralph, along with Carmelita being turned over to Manny and Jonas. The times Ross had spent in Yuma had been a little tumultuous in the early years. But after Jason Grant had been restored to his prison cell and Jeremy Grant and his henchmen died everything had settled down.

He and Flora had a wonderful run of years, a son who was a marvel as far as Ross was concerned, and the friendship of the man and his wife who was rid-ing alongside him again. He counted Yuma as per-haps the best place he had ever lived. Ralph had mixed feelings about the years he had spent in Yuma, but certainly not those during which he and Ross had spent so much time together.

As they drew near to Yuma, riding just outside the heavy brush line along the Colorado River, they began to see the dust cloud the town raised. Though there were a few of the new-fangled things called automobiles in the area mostly the people still rode horses or walked wherever they went. As people walked they kicked up dust. As the horses walked or trotted, or even galloped, they kicked up dust. Everything going on in the town seemed to kick up dust. There were no "paved" streets in Yuma though paving of streets was being considered by the "Town Fathers."

The air around the entire town was a kind of light brown colored miasma which resembled a fog. On the worst days it was necessary to wear a bandanna over your nose to filter out some of the grit. Rinsing out your mouth with water, or beer, or some other form of liquid refreshment was a constant necessity. The fog of dust did not change very often. When it did there was probably a wind storm in progress and the density of the dirt in the air grew thicker. They saw the dust for miles in their trek, reminding Ross of his ride into Yuma from Wellton, and then suddenly they were enveloped within the miasma and very shortly came into the center of town.

Ralph and Ross rode directly to the sheriff's office, gave up their handguns and rifles and headed for the Palace. A deputy was on duty with whom they were not acquainted. All he said, other than "Here are your receipts," was 'I think the sheriff will want to talk with you men. I am not sure when he will be back in town, or if he is back already, but I will tell him you are here if I see him before you."

They rode their horses around the backside of the Palace to the small livery and stable area behind the building, knowing it was there. They took care of their horses, before doing anything else, rubbing them down, feeding them some grain, seeing to it there was plenty of hay in their feed troughs, and water in the water trough, brushed them a little and then went in the back door of the Palace. The time they spent with the horses was not just out of their respect for their animals. It was born of the knowledge they would most likely be aboard the horses backs for another trek very soon.

As they came into the lobby of the hotel the desk clerk, who had worked there for many years, yelled out, "Mr. Ross, Mr. Ralph oh it's so good to see you." Then his face changed and he took a different mien as he came out from behind the desk, shook their hands and patted them on the arms, each in turn, and said "I'm so terribly sorry for why you have to be here. She was such a lovely girl and so good to work for and with here in this place. She treated us all so well…" A tear fell down his cheeks and he unabashedly cried a little as he stepped back behind the registration desk. His name was Harley.

"Thank you, Harley" Ralph said. "Thank you very much. It is good to see your face as well my old friend. The times have been good to you." Ross tipped his hat to Harley though he said nothing. Emotions were hard for Ross to bear. He brushed away a tear as Harley went back behind his desk. Ralph heard a commotion coming from the bar, and saw Jonas headed for the two of them.

When the clerk greeted Ralph and Ross, Jonas, who had heard the clerk, made his way to the lobby of the hotel from the saloon after asking Jake to take over behind the bar. He bumped into a table and chair he was so focused on Ralph and Ross, making a racket. He saw his father standing next to Ross in the lobby and walked directly to him. He looked at Ralph and extended his hand and said "Sir, Dad, I'm so happy you are here." As Ralph grasped Jonas hand and drew his son to him Jonas, who had held his feelings in check for a lot of days, broke down and sobbed for a time. Ralph and Ross wrapped their arms around him and did basically the same thing as Harley joined them all of them crying unabashedly.

When the keening stopped the hotel clerk offered them hotel towels with which to dry their eyes and take care of any other difficulties created by the emotions. None of these men of the west, these "tough guys," were used to the emotions they had just released. None of them were used to allowing themselves what they saw as the luxury of exhibiting such feelings, but the worst was yet to come.

Realizing Manny was not there, not among them, Ross asked, "Where is he?" Ross asked. "Where is my other son?"

Neither Ralph nor Jonas blanched or reacted to Ross's question and statement. Both Ross and Ralph felt they were brothers by other mothers. Jonas was brought into their relationship as naturally as was Manny. answered Manny was asleep. Jonas explained to Ross the doctor kept Manny full of laudanum for a couple of days and Jonas kept him drunk enough to sleep for the last several days. He said, "I didn't feed him the liquor. I would have, to protect him for a time, but he did it on his own." Jonas told them he could not function and run the place without Manny being asleep.

If Manny was awake he was sitting in the saloon drinking and if he was in the bar he was also crying.

It was destructive of business as people, though they sympathized with why it was happening, wanted to shy away from Manny as he cried and keened over Janie. Jonas also told Ross it was difficult to see him completely devastated as he was. It was easier, for the moment, if Jonas just let Manny get drunk real fast every morning and then put him to bed. Jonas said, "He should be waking up in an hour or so. Let him sleep for now. The three of us need to talk anyway. It will be a difficult moment for him to see you, and for you to see the state he is in."

But they did not get out of the hallway between the saloon and the hotel before Manny appeared, a little groggy, stumbling a little, swaying more than he should but aware enough to know his father was there. "Oh God, Dad," he cried out, "the son-of-a-bitch shot my Janie. How could he have shot her? How could God have permitted her to die? Shit, it should have been me, God knows it should have been me. It was me he wanted, the son of a bitch." Manny almost collapsed. Ralph and Ross semi-carried him into the saloon. Henry brought a wet towel to wipe the tears and sleep from Manny' eyes. Jonas went to get them all some cold beer and set ups for what he anticipated would be several shots of whiskey each.

When he got back to the table Ross was patting Manny in the face lightly and saying "Come on son, snap out of it for a bit. Come on, son. We need to talk man to man. Come on, son." It seemed Manny was having a hard time getting through the fog of sleep and booze, the cycle he had been in for days on end. Jake the barman brought Ross some ice chips in a towel. Ross put them on the back of Manny's neck and rubbed the cold into Manny's skin there. In a moment or two Manny began to be more lucid and awake. He said to Ross with only a little bit of a quavering voice, "Okay Dad. I'm okay. I promise, and I don't need a drink for a while, Jonas," he said to Jonas as the beers and drinks arrived at the table.

Jonas said, "I didn't bring you any, brother. I know you don't need any more." Jonas passed beers to Ross and Ralph and sat one down for himself along with a bottle of good whiskey and several shot glasses he had brought along. Manny stared at them all and didn't say anything. He wanted a drink in the worst way, just to dull his senses, to be able to forget, but he didn't take one. No one would have faulted him had he done so, and no one would have stopped him. He knew those things were true, but he didn't take one. It was a moment he would remember, indeed they all would, for the rest of his life. His mind cleared a little more minute by minute as he waited for the opportunity to discuss how they would catch and punish Martin.

All save for Manny, including Harley and Jake, sipped beer for a moment and then Jonas began to tell them what he had learned about where Martin was and how he had gotten the information. The tale of Jonas being prepared to kill someone if necessary or to beat the crap out of someone to learn of Martin's whereabouts was tragically funny. Ross smiled as Jonas related the events. Out of pure happenstance while the four of them were seated at a table with Jake hovering around them, Henry Fellows walked in the front door of the Palace. Jake saw a man who was far more likely to be in the Cactus Bar than in the Palace and started to move toward him.

Jonas turned slightly, saw Henry walk in, saw Jake headed toward him, and spoke loudly to all. "Jake," who stopped, hearing his name called by Jonas, "I want you to meet Henry Fellows. Henry, please come in, please join us. Jake would you please make a set up for Henry." Jonas turned to the rest at the table and said, "This is the man I told you about, the man in Cactus Bar who had the courage and the will to tell me where Robert Martin was located." Jake arrived with the set up for Henry and Jonas said, "Henry will always be welcome here, at any rate he will for so long as I have anything to say about it." Having said those things Jonas turned and introduced Henry, one by one, to Ross, Manny, Ralph, Jake and Harley, inviting Henry to sit down next to him.

Jonas proposed a toast to Henry's courage and willingness to see the horror in Robert Martin's actions even though he counted Martin as a long-time friend. After the men had raised their glasses and solemnly imbibed, Henry said, "It is the reason I am here today Jonas. I had a short letter from Martin and I wanted you to see it. He is unrepentant and confirms his desire to see you and Manny, Ralph and Ross dead. Here is the letter, you can read it for yourself."

Jonas read out loud going through a paragraph of badly phrased language which Martin said was being written for him. The second paragraph contained the piece to which Henry referred. It was not long but it was challenging. Jonas read it aloud also. "I hope you show this to Jonas and Manny. I want to kill them. If I can get them to come over here to Calipatria I will kill them. Tell them to come on. I am ready for them, the bastards, Oh yeah I hope those two pieces of dog dung, their fathers, come along as well. All of them can die together."

It was very quiet at the table for a moment. Ralph, whose patience levels were, all those years after chasing down Jason Grant, still a little lacking, said, "Well shit then let's go get the guy and bring him back to be tried or if he tries to fight we'll just kill him there and bring back his body for the undertaker to display."

Manny immediately stood up and said "Okay, I am damn sure ready to go but Robert Martin is not going to return to Yuma for trial. I am going to hang him with my bare hands. If I ever see his face again it will be the last moments of his life when I do." Ralph thought to himself, well, I asked the question of myself on the ride up here. Now I know the answer for sure. He wants revenge and as it stands right now nothing else is going to satisfy him unless it is Robert Martin's death.

"I taught you better Manny," Ross said. "Sit down. We are not going anywhere for a while. For one thing my horse and Ralph's need rest. We could not ride them across the street without taking the chance of one or both going down, and all of us know the consequences of that happening. We are not going anywhere for a while. Now sit down son. We need to talk and begin to form a plan. Ralph you know better than anyone here other than me we can't go off half-cocked, shit and so do you Manny."

Jonas said nothing during the time Ross was talking. As usual Jonas was the more deliberate of the younger men. He was in fact more like Ross than he was like his own father. He had often considered his patience to be because of his Army experience.

He said, "No one I know has ever been to Calipatria. I don't even know what the hell they are mining in the area. I don't know anything about the countryside at all. I think you are right Uncle Ross, we need to take it easy for a day or two and let you and Ralph's horses rest. While we are getting ready we can try to get some information, some more information, some way to devise a plan. We cannot simply go riding into Calipatria with gun's blazing for the very least reason because there is the likelihood is the guy has some friends there. Assuming he does more people will get hurt than really should. We also need to get provisions together for the trip. It is a fair distance over there to be sure." Jonas looked at Henry for a moment.

Henry felt the weight of Jonas' stare and said, "I have never been to Calipatria but it is on the other side of El Centro and north of there I think. This I do know about Martin. He has a lot of friends over there. He bragged about his buddies being tough men all the time when he was here. You can bet he will have plenty of help. One thing I will tell you because I have been to El Centro and it is the sheriff there is insistent about guns. He does not allow anyone to wear them in his town, period. You might expect some trouble from him."

Ralph looked at his son Jonas admiringly but jokingly, he said, "Who are you, and where is my son?" Everyone laughed at the comment. Everyone also knew Jonas's comment bore with it the truth.

With the tension lifted a little they all had a beer and a shot of whiskey or two to go along with. Manny stayed away from the booze even though the other three sampled the whiskey bottle several times while drinking their beer. Manny wanted to be alert and to participate in the discussion of what they were going to do as fully as was possible. Ralph asked Jonas during what was a bit of a lull in the conversation, "How well do you know the sheriff, son?"

"Dad, I know him pretty well, but I don't think he can help us. He has only been here about five years and he came from points east as I recall. I doubt he knows much about California if anything. Also, he has no ability to help us outside the town or outside Yuma County. He might be able to send a letter along with us asking we be permitted to bring Martin back."

Manny said, "Who do you think could give us additional information Jonas?"

"I don't know right now," Jonas answered, "but I am thinking on it and tomorrow will be another day. I will ask around town tomorrow, go back down to the Cactus and talk to those guys down there if I have to and of course I will talk to the sheriff."

As they sat at the table Manny would begin to leak tears now and again. Usually he would just wipe them off his face on his sleeve. After watching this occur several times Jake came over with a bar towel and handed it to Manny and said "Just keep this Manny and when you are done with it I will put it in the wash. Oh, I almost forgot, Jonas, have you gotten anyone else to do the wash yet?" Janie had overseen getting the wash done in the bar and hotel. She hired people to do the work from among those in the town who she learned needed work.

Jonas replied, "No, but Helen is looking at a couple of women in town who are having a hard time. She thinks there are several who might do it. I will get back with her tonight and see what she says. I know it's beginning to stack up back there, and if we can't find anyone I will get it done one way or another to-morrow."

Manny had listened to all this knowing his Janie had overseen the laundry, feeling her loss in a new way. "It's all right Jonas," Manny said. "I will get up early tomorrow and do it myself if Helen doesn't get someone. It will give me something to do besides sit on my bed and look at the ceiling seeing the face of my beautiful Janie in front of my eyes, dead." Everyone was stunned for a moment.

"My God, son," Ross said, "you have to start to cope with this. It's very hard. I know it is. When Jenny died it was nearly as hard on your mother and I as it was on Ralph. We loved her. Flora was almost as much a mother to her as was Georgi." Ralph nodded vigorously. "We all had a terrible time for a little bit but we had to go on and you do too son. We all loved Janie too. She was a wonderful girl and I wish you could have had many years with her. But it was not to be. You must go on now son. You must get a grip on yourself and begin to make a life for yourself again."

"I know Dad. It's very hard. If I had not been there, if I had not seen the light go out of her lovely blue eyes, if I had not felt the life go out of her wonderful little body maybe I could cope better, but I was there, and I did feel those things happen, and I cannot stop thinking about it. Oh shit." Again, Manny broke down. Ross put his arm on Manny's shoulders and held him close as his son sobbed away again for a while holding the towel which had started it all to his face.

Ross told Manny, when the crying was over again, "You will have the opportunity to turn this to anger for a moment Manny. But you cannot let it eat you up and become a desire for nothing but vengeance. Remember, son this started by Martin as an act of vengeance, a misplaced sense of loyalty was the basis for this man to try and shoot you. You must let go of the idea of revenge. It can only turn you into another Robert Martin. If you can give up on the idea of revenge, it means Manny, look at me son, it means if we can capture him and bring him back to be tried and sentenced here in Yuma then it is what we do. He will have no one to buy the judge like Jeremy Grant did for the sentencing of Jason Grant. A trial will most likely mean a death sentence and your vengeance will be wrought by the state. Then you can forget the Martin family forever. I know you don't want to hear those things but we have to do this right son."

"But I'll never forget what he did to my Janie."

"Of course not Manny my son, nor should you ever forget," Ralph said. "I can speak to the notion of never forgetting more clearly than Ross I expect. I will tell you right now if I could go out to the territorial prison and drag Jason Grant out of his cell I would personally tie him up like a pig and hang him very slowly from a short tree. As he swung there, choking with a loose rope tightening on him, I would cut off his balls and his dick just to complete my revenge." Ross shuddered when Ralph said those things because he knew that Ralph meant every word.

"But what would I accomplish if I did hang him Manny? I would end up in prison too, wouldn't I? Would it be a positive from the standpoint of my having revenge? No, it would not and neither will it be a positive if we must leave you in a California jail because you have killed the Martin boy prematurely. I hate Jason Grant with every fiber of my being Manny, my son. I would not kill him, not if push came to shove. No, I would not kill him. Just as I did so many years ago now, I would take him back to serve the rest of his sentence. Oh, I wanted to just pull the trigger and get rid of him. You should know I did. I'm sure Ross does. I didn't and I was justified. He was shooting at me. He missed. I could have shot him right then and there and no one, well, only me would have quibbled with my decision. Wait. I'm not done."

Ralph paused, took a long drink from his beer, flashed down a shot of the Palace's good whiskey and then looked intently at Manny and said, "You must make up your mind your revenge will be to watch Martin get his neck stretched by the territory of Arizona. Always remember Manny revenge is a dish best served cold. The heat of anger only creates more reaction and more revenge. Your attitude must be cold and calculating. You must allow someone else to complete your revenge. It will a little less satisfying but you will be able to look yourself in the mirror every day and say, okay, he got his but it was not me which brought it down on him. It was the law."

Jonas and Ross looked at each other and Jonas said, lifting his glass to his father, "I think that is the longest speech I have ever seen you make Dad." Jonas smiled and it was returned by his father. All of them nodded agreement with Ralph and looked at Manny to know for sure he understood. He nodded his head and took up a glass of beer Ross had requested Jake bring for him. They all sipped on their beer, reflecting on Ralph's speech, impressed, knowing he had hit the nail on the head.

Ross smiled and tipped his hat as he stood up, and he said, "I remember this place has the best baths of any I ever have been in. I need a bath. I need to get the trail dust of me and my clothes. Manny, I want to have you see to it my clothes are cleaned, and son, you should change those you have on and have them cleaned as well." Manny nodded his understanding. His dad was giving him something to occupy his time. Ross also said, "After my bath I am going to take a room in this hotel and go to sleep for about a day. I am getting too damned old to sit the saddle as long as we did Ralph." They all smiled and Ross went in and rented rooms for he and Ralph.

Manny took his fathers (he considered the two of them to be a father to him in reality) to the baths and took both Ross's and Ralph's clothes to be cleaned, steamed and pressed right away. While on the way to the baths he stopped in his suite and changed clothes himself. He left the hotel to go to the store down the street to get the clothes done. As he walked people came up to him and said several times, "We are so sorry for your loss Manny. She was a lovely girl." He thanked them all and managed to make it all the way to the cleaners before crying again.

Ralph and Ross were clean, their clothes were clean, they had breakfast in a little cafe close by to the saloon and came back to find Manny and Jonas seated in the saloon having coffee together. Ross and Ralph sat down and asked Jake to get them some coffee as well. Ross said, "Do we know how far it is to El Centro?"

Jonas answered, "It's somewhere around sixty to eighty miles I am told. Henry Fellows has been there many times and he told me he thought it was at least two, maybe three days riding."

"All right then we should count on it being about a three to four-day ride and we might be pushing it a little to do it in three days. We do not need to push the horses harder than necessary. We will need the horses when we get to Calipatria for sure. Is there any water on the way there other than the Colorado River?"

Manny answered the question Ross raised by saying "No, I don't think so. Some of the drummers who come into the saloon have talked about what a long dry trip it is here from El Centro. I guess it means we must carry water bags with enough water for the horses for at least four days. We should be able to get water in El Centro when we get there I would think." In the back of Ross's mind a concern was raised about the town of El Centro. They could not skirt the town because it was the only place to get water and some food. All would be clear when they arrived in El Centro.

"Yes, it should be fine and if we do it in three days we will have extra water. We will have to take canteens for us as well since we will need water for us and most of all for coffee in the mornings."

The four of them spent a lot of time going through the whole litany of how much food to take, whether they were likely to see any game, with Manny saying there was not likely to be any game, based on knowledge gained from drummers. They decided the kind of arms they would carry. Ross asked if guns were prohibited in El Centro. No one at the table knew and neither did anyone working in the hotel or the saloon. Jonas had a thought and sent Jake down to the Cactus to see if anyone there knew about the issue of gun control in El Centro. When Jake came back he said, "No one down there knew for sure but all of them thought there wasn't any law against packing a pistol or a rifle."

They decided to take saddle bags full of hard tack and pemmican, at least one day of clean clothing and plenty of ammunition as well as a few other amenities like a coffee pot and some plates to eat on if they should find some game. They would pack all those things on one horse which none of them would ride. The pack horse would also carry some wood for a fire each evening.

They decided to let the horses eat and water up for the next two days. They would leave Yuma two days later. They also decided Manny would be the only one of them who would not pack a gun all the time. During the ride he would be armed. Going into El Centro he would be unarmed. Going into Calipatria he would be unarmed. They hoped by leaving him unarmed in El Centro and Calipatria way they could make sure that he didn't just shoot the guy at first sighting. He agreed to the idea because he was afraid he would not be able to contain himself with Martin if he saw him or they captured him.

With all the decisions made the four of them sat and talked quietly of the times of Ross and Ralph and of how things had been with Manny and Janie, and how things had been with Jonas and Manny and the Palace. The flow of people in and out of the saloon was a pretty good indicator of how well the place was doing. The business was constant. The customers were never a mass of people and they were never raucous or out of line, well almost never. Thankfully the days of "hoorawing" saloons had died with the death of the large trail herds from Texas to Kansas. Cowboys being paid monthly was the same throughout the country and their drunken brawls, and the lack of gun control in earlier days produced shooting of lamps, mirrors, pianos, anything which drew their attention. The last of those kinds of events in the Palace had been many years earlier.

The four of them talked about who would run the business while they were on their trip. Jake would run the bar and pull in another guy to help with the bartending he knew. The hotel desk clerk was fully capable of running the hotel and they would leave it to him for the days they were gone. They sent wires to be taken to Flora and Carmella they were needed in Yuma and please come as soon as they could but not to hurry.

The business would not be a distraction, a problem. When they got back from Calipatria they expected Flora and Carmella to be there and be in charge. Everyone in Yuma knew by now where Martin was. When the four saddled up two days later and they headed for the ferry to cross the Colorado River along with their pack horse, they were seen. Everyone in town would take care of the Palace as well. It would not be a problem at all. The four put it out of their minds. The problem they had to deal with was far more concerning than the business.

What would they face when they got to Calipatria. Martin's braggadocio about having a lot of friends could mean some serious trouble, could mean they would be involved in a serious gun battle. Perhaps, just perhaps, the men of the mines in Calipatria would see Martin for what he was, a back shooter who had killed a pregnant woman. If so much trouble might be avoided, but it was necessary they be ready. Each carried plenty of extra ammunition for each of their weapons.

7

El Centro, Growth

Early November 1910

It was a fateful, cold, and windy day in November 1910 when four men rode out of Yuma together. Two fathers and two sons rode side by each in the fashion of the Army, two by two with the pack horse trailing Manny to start out the trip. They would alternate having the pack horse behind them, meaning they would alternate being in a lead or following position. The horses were at a trot until they reached the ferry crossing the Colorado River.

137

Each man wore a pistol or two. Ross Hendershot wore two, one on his left hip as ever and one in a shoulder holster. He also carried a Henry repeating rifle loaded with fifteen rounds of 44-40 ammunition. The two pistols he wore were Colt manufactured, called by virtually all western men Peacemakers, in .45 caliber. He had, in his time, used both pistols with lethal results.

At Ross's left side rode his son Manny. Manny, only past 19 years of age, married and widowed already, who had begun to practice firing a pistol when he was a mere lad of five years of age. Ross taught him well. He also taught Manny how to load, how to clean the pistol, and rifle, how to oil it and keep the holster in which it rode, the holster kept supple with its own kind of oil applied.

Manny wore, on this day, a Colt .45 Peacemaker as well, and under his right leg rode a scabbard with a .56 caliber Sharps Buffalo gun in it. The rifle belonged to Ross. It had a long scope on the stock and the first part of the barrel and the gun was accurate to a range of well over five hundred yards in the hands of most. In Ross's hands it had been used once at nearly a thousand yards successfully, meaning a man who had just tried to kill him died after being struck by a bullet from the Sharps.

Ralph Forney rode just behind and to the right of Ross. Ralph was armed similarly to Ross but he also carried his favorite weapon in a scabbard which was tied onto the back of his saddle, it being a double barreled twelve-gauge shotgun loaded with heavy shot. When it became appropriate he intended to sling it under his duster as always. The sling allowed him to simply drop the stock into his left hand and fire it either one barrel at a time or both at once. Its effect was devastating at close range. Ross had seen the results first hand when two men named Ringo and Borland had tried to kill him and Ralph in the Palace saloon one day. Ralph also carried a Henry fifteen shot repeating rifle under his right leg in a scabbard.

It was said about the Henry, chambered in 44-40 caliber rounds, it could be fired, you could lay the weapon down, pick up a pair of binoculars and watch the round hit about two hundred yards away. But Ralph and Ross, using the Henry rifles they carried, had destroyed the front of the home of Jeremy Grant one fine morning, blowing the door off its hinges, breaking all the windows and poking large holes in the exterior front wall. Ralph knew it to be a devastating weapon at the right range.

Jonas Forney was the fourth of this group and he rode just slightly to the right of and behind his father. The four rode purposefully, at least at first they did, and quickly, pushing their horses a little in the initial parts of the ride. But this was not a sprint, this was a marathon. Jonas was armed with a Colt's pistol also but it was in .44 caliber and shot the same bullet basically as the Henry repeater which rode under his right leg in a scabbard. Jonas had been a scout in the southeastern part of Arizona during the late times of the Apache wars toward the end of the 19th century. He rode easily at a trot he could maintain on his horse for hours on end. Of the four of them it had been the longest time since Manny had taken a ride of any duration. Manny sat in his saddle a little uneasily for a short time and then began to sit back and enjoy the ride.

About a mile into the ride after crossing the Colorado River on the ferry, Ross slowed Roan II down and patted his horse's neck and gave him his head. They were pointed basically toward the west, on a path with the sun in the morning at their back. The trail they would follow was well defined with deep wagon ruts. It had been used in the travels of hundreds of drummers and pilgrims through the years. They would deviate slightly from the trail to avoid the soft and seriously dusty sugar sand areas. Those were extremely difficult for the horses to walk in and the dust kicked up in those areas was enough to choke the horses, never mind the men, so the four would ride out away from the beaten track.

The desert between Yuma and El Centro is extremely barren. There are only a few trees and they are spread out, miles and miles apart. One of the areas which the men needed to traverse was a set of sugar sand dunes, some rising to forty feet high and higher. The sand dunes extended south and west toward El Centro and started about ten to fifteen miles to the west of Yuma. The trail skirted the south edges of the dunes. It was possible, though not advisable, to cross the dunes on horseback. Jonas, in his conversations with several who traveled back and forth some was told they should stay to the south edges. Any other choices could get them lost, never to be seen again. The skirted the dunes.

There was very little vegetation but apparently enough for some animals to survive eating the tufts of grass or creosote leaves. In some areas the creosote bushes were ubiquitous with their dangerously sharp center root balls exposed. The trail meandered through those spots appearing to go in almost every direction but in the final analysis constantly bearing west. It was warm during the day and cooled off to very temperate nights. Breaks had to be given to the horses as they proceeded, also giving the men a break from the swaying gaits of the horses.

All four men were dressed similarly in dark pants and white shirt, a coat like that of a suit coat, a white duster over those clothes, and a vest under the suit coat. The duster was useless for each of them since they wore it open. The duster had to be open to give them access to their weapons. It was not only due to the possibility, however slight it might be, of trouble with another human being along the way, but it was also due to their desire to be able to hunt small game or even a deer if one happened along during their trip.

Each of the men rode in a kind of dead space of their own, spread out slightly to avoid the dust of the man in front of them or their own, giving mind to the wind direction always and again both for the avoidance of dust and the possibility of small game appearing along the way. Each of the men rode with their own thoughts though generally focused simply on the task at hand, crossing a difficult stretch of dangerous terrain.

Manny's thoughts were on Janie constantly, and even while riding he cried. He tried to keep it as quiet as possible in order not to disturb anyone else. It did not occur every minute of the ride but was an intermittent distraction to him. He tried to focus on nothing but the ride and failed. She was only days in the ground after all. He kept a towel in front of him tucked in under one leg to wipe away his tears and on which to blow his nose. All noticed what was going on but said nothing. It was their way, their life experience to give each man with which they rode whatever leeway he needed personally. But it was also their relationships which brought them to make sure he was moving with the rest of them while knowing his heart was elsewhere.

As they rode the all watched for signs of trouble, looked for signs of animals, looked for possible shady spots in which to let the horses relax after a time. Since the desert in that area was barren but for creosote bushes which didn't grow high nor grow enough limbs and foliage to provide shade, they looked for an indentation in the ground, maybe a sand wash in which the banks might provide a little shade.

There was little conversation during the ride. There was no need for any further conversation out of the normal. The four were on a mission. Their task was clear, capture and return Martin to Arizona. Short of capturing and returning him they would kill him if necessary. Several hours into the ride Ross pulled the reins in on Roan II, stopped and dismounted and began to walk alongside his horse. The rest followed suit.

They came to a sand wash which was barely visible to any of them until they arrived at its location. Ross led them down a small trail into the wash and settled down in the shade on the east side of the wash where the sun was behind him. Roan II wandered a little way away, his reins trailing, but staying mostly in the shade as well. All the horses followed Roan, feeding on small desert grasses. They would not go far and would find shade of their own.

Ralph shook his head at Ross and said, "How the hell did you see this sand wash, pard?"

Ross answered, "It looked like a line in the dirt to me as we were riding toward it."

Jonas volunteered, "When I first went to tracking the Army people would tell me, thinking I was nothing but a greenhorn kid. It was true, but I learned. If you are at a trot or a gallop and you see a line in the dirt slow down because you are coming up on a sand wash. I guess it is what you meant Ross?"

"Yes, Jonas, yes it was. I learned about it when I was riding from Phoenix to Yuma primarily. I got shot at by a posse of non-lawmen who were chasing a group of five rustlers. I saw a line in the dirt as I rode away from them and went for it, and it turned out to be a sand wash. I have remembered the appearance ever since."

Manny had wandered down the sand wash, walking away from the other three. They thought he was going to use the desert as a repository for some body water, as each of them would do in time. He was, but on his walk down the wash to a more private spot he saw a rabbit, quickly drew his pistol and shot the rabbit. As he came back the other three all had guns out, ready for anything. He was carrying the rabbit by the legs. He had already gutted it and skinned it.

He showed it to Jonas who looked at the neck and saw something move there. Jonas immediately cut off the head and the front quarters of the rabbit. When Manny asked why Jonas took the head and neck area and sliced into it to show Manny the worms in the neck. There was no way to preserve the meat left after the removal of the front quarter so they cut strips off it and made a small but very hot fire in a hasty manner, cooked the meat, salted it and hung it in strips from a piece of mesquite. They would munch on those pieces of meat as they went along. The break from the ride was lengthened by the process but they were in no hurry. No one complained, especially not Manny since it was he who had taken the rabbit.

While the rabbit was cooking Ross and Ralph tended to all five horses. They gave each horse at least a hat full of water and a little grain. Ross had taken several apples from a bag which normally was kept in the livery behind the Palace. He cut two of them into quarters and fed them to the horses. When the rabbit was done they walked the horses out of the sand wash and then mounted to ride on. Again, they trotted the horses for about a half an hour and then started the slow walking gait which ate up territory so fast. At the end of the first day they built a fire, sat around it and ate strips of rabbit meat, pemmican and hardtack washed down with a little water for each of them. It had been a good day. They all bedded down on the desert floor and slept well.

Just before dawn each day they were on the trail Ross rose, stirred the fire and put a little more wood on it, got out the coffee pot and started the coffee brewing. Ralph was always awake but offered no help. It had always been a kind of agreement between them while on the trail as a division of labors of a sort.

If anyone wanted to eat in the morning it would have to be hardtack and pemmican. The rabbit was small and the meat disappeared the first day. There would be no more game meat for the rest of their trek to the west. By dawn of the second day, all four were full of coffee which was brewing before any-one besides Ross was up and around, a few pieces of pemmican mixed with a little water to make it more palatable and hardtack and they were in the saddle and on their way. They left their first camp slowly in the dark, letting the horses pick their way toward the far horizon with the light of dawn slowly ascending over the mountains behind them. Every morning it was the same for three days.

The morning of the fourth day began with a few differences. As the dawn began to spring upon them Ross, Ralph, Jonas and Manny were checking their weapons. Ross took Manny's pistol from him and said "I will give this back to you a little later son, but let's get into El Centro and make sure Martin is not there before you take it back. But son if you want to promise me, to swear to me you wouldn't shoot Martin you can just keep it."

Manny just nodded, made no promises, said nothing more. He didn't trust himself not to shoot Martin at first sight. As each day of the ride had progressed he had become a little less remorseful about Janie's death and a little angrier at her murderer. He simply didn't know whether he could see the man and not kill him.

It wasn't a matter of trust for Ross, it was common sense which said don't let my son be guilty of a crime and end up in prison himself. Ross had seen the metamorphosis of his son's attitude in the last few days. He knew Manny's attitude toward Martin was becoming more and more about hatred, about desire to kill. Manny knew his father's motivation. He was acquiescent if not happy about the situation. It made little difference to Manny. He could and would, if it came to it, tear Martin to pieces, literally, with his bare hands.

As the four men began their ride on the fourth day they could see El Centro's dust on the horizon. The dust cloud in the air meant El Centro could be no more than a few miles away at most. The four rode on, now riding abreast, Manny next to his father. Ross wore Manny's gun in his belt, and was ready to toss it to Manny at any point in time if need be. As the four rode toward El Centro they could also see a dust trail which seemed to be headed toward them. It turned out to be one man. He was a deputy sheriff and his name was Shamus King.

As Shamus rode up to the four they spread a little further apart so they would not be a mass target but individual targets instead. Shamus pulled up to a halt in front of them, in the middle of the four, roughly, and almost directly opposite of Ross. He was armed and his gun was not tied down. Since he had on a tin star shining brightly in the sun Ross did not take his tie down off his own weapon. It was a way of showing neutral intent even in the face of potential hostility. He introduced himself and then he said, "Hi gents. We have heard of your coming by the way. My sheriff will want your weapons before you can come into El Centro. Which of you is Manny Hendershot?"

Ralph said, "We have no reason nor desire to break the law Mr. King, but we will not give up our weapons until we are in your town. We intend to ride there protected from any potential for ambush by the coward named Robert Martin. If you and your sheriff are supporting Mr. Martin then we will probably fight right here and now. If your intent is to stop us from protecting ourselves from a back-shooting coward who kills young women I expect you better move out of our way now, sir. One more thing sir, I remind you the law out here in the desert is not the same as in your city and you have no authority out here. If your intent is to make us vulnerable to attack then you are on wrong track, mister. My question is do we need to kill you here and now or will you permit us to ride into your city with our guns where they are located presently?"

Having said those things Ralph very ostentatiously removed the tie downs from the hammers of both his pistols and Ross and Jonas followed suit. It was very clear to King these men were ready for a fight given the right circumstance. He looked at them and saw death in the eyes of Jonas, the youngest. He thought, my God, these men would kill me with no caring at all. He was a hard man himself but he had never seen another man which showed him the devil was standing next to his side.

King shook his head for a moment, put his right hand in the air so it was clear he was not reaching for a weapon, looked at Ross and said, "You would be Hendershot Sr. I guess." He looked at Manny and said, "You have the looks of your father so I am guessing you are Manny Hendershot. I am terribly sorry for your loss Mr. Manny Hendershot. My whole town is sorry for your loss. But Mr. Hendershot Sr., and I assume your friend who spoke to me so harshly is Mr. Forney, we do not intend to have a shoot-out on our streets occur in this century ever. Do I make myself clear?"

Ross, speaking low but with his intent clear, responded, "Do you intend to try and stop us crossing the rest of the desert to your town with our arms on our bodies?"

"No sir. But there are about fifty men between here and El Centro. If you men try to go into our town with those guns on you will be shot down in cold blood. Do I make myself clear?" King's attitude by then had become antagonistic, even challenging. He had become angry in part because of his fear. Not many men concerned him enough to cause him fear.

"Yes, you do deputy. Make no mistake here. We have no grief with any of those men nor with your town unless you are harboring Martin. You know who we are seeking. Is he in your town?" Ross asked. Everyone had hands on guns by then except King whose right hand still was palm forward in the air. The tensions had mounted with each passing sentence or so it seemed. Ross continued and said, "If Robert Martin is in your town and you are harboring him Mr. King, then you and every one of your fifty men is dead as we speak. It is only a matter of when they are shot. Are you ready to die for Robert Martin, Mr. King? Are you ready to see fifty men from your town die for protecting Robert Martin, Mr. King?"

The tone of Ross's remarks had, by the time those comments were uttered, changed from conciliatory, even friendly at first, to openly hostile. It was clear to King Ross and the others were ready to go to war if need be.

The deputy, sensing these men had reached a point where they would no longer be ordered nor provoked, said, "No Mr. Hendershot he is not in our town. We have seen to it, and he is gone. No one must die here today Mr. Hendershot. You will be welcome there, all of you, but not with guns on. I will ride with you and tell you when you must disarm yourselves. We are not harboring Robert Martin. We do not want a war with you men. Are those terms acceptable to all four of you?" As challenging as he had been initially

King's mien had changed to a much more conciliatory tone.

Surprising Ross and Ralph both to a degree, "Your offer is a great compromise," Manny said. "I am unarmed now. The rest of us will disarm the minute you tell us it is appropriate unless we see someone is about to draw down on us. Then, Mr. King I can assure you what my father just said is what will happen. You could have a hundred and fifty men between here and hell and they would all die if you were harboring Robert Martin. Dad, Ralph, Jonas, do you agree?" Each nodded their head. "But make no mistake about this deputy, Robert Martin will be captured and taken back to Yuma for trial, or if he forces us to do so we will kill him," Manny added.

"Okay then, let's go," Shamus said, shaking his head, thinking to himself, I could have made this a lot easier from the outset.

The five of them had ridden about two hundred yards when ten men came out of a small sand wash on horseback. It was evident they had been laying down in the wash with their horses prone as well. The horses were shaking off the dust and dirt. The riders were armed and alert. The deputy said to them, "It's all right. Pull in behind us a hundred yards or so and follow us into town." The riders did as he said. As the group of five grew nearer to town the same thing happened several times until there was a large body of men behind the five. Each time this sort of thing happened Ross just shook his head.

Ralph, looking back on this group at one point mumbled, "What the hell did you people think we were gonna do, burn your town down? If it is what you thought you have no idea who we are or what we are about. Ross's reputation and mine alone should have told you we represented no threat to your town."

The deputy was riding closest to Ross, between Ross and Manny, but heard Ralph's comment. He slowed his horse and looked at Ralph and said, "No Mr. Forney, we didn't think you were going to burn our town down. We knew sure as hell you were not going to do damage to our town as you can see. What we did think was if Robert Martin was in our town you would murder him on our streets and we could not let something along those lines happen either."

Manny got angry then. He shouted at the deputy. "Murder, what the hell do you mean murder? The son-of-a-bitch deserves anything he gets. He shot my wife and killed my baby. Why the hell are you bastards defending him? Shit. You are an asshole Mr. King. I would just as lief have it out with you right this damned second you bastard."

By the time Manny was finished the deputy was red in the face but sat quietly for a moment. One of the men from the group behind who heard Manny's outburst yelled out "You are right Hendershot, but by God it will not happen in our town."

"Does that answer your question Mr. Hendershot?" the deputy asked.

"It answers my question, but it is not appropriate for you people to be harboring a fugitive from justice or preventing us from taking him back to Yuma to be tried for the murder of my wife and child. If it is what you people are about we will eventually have war with you one way or another. Do you want to start right now deputy? I see your anger but by God you have not lost your wife of only three months or so dying in your arms as you watched the light go out in her eyes, knowing your child was dying with her. You ready to go right now you son of bitch?"

"You are right of course Mr. Hendershot, I have not suffered those losses, but I assure you we are not harboring Mr. Martin. He is not welcome in our town any more than you are if you are armed. Now we are in the area on the outskirts of our town where we want your guns so turn them over unless you want to start a war right here. Oh yes, Mr. Hendershot I do not want to have a fight with you today. But if you do not give up your guns we will fight."

Manny, still angry and willing to go to war, said, "Then you would die." King's neck flamed red but he did nothing overt to start a gun battle. He simply gestured to Ross.

Ross said, "You may have our guns for as long as we are in your town. I assume that you will allow us to re-provision before you require us to float. We need water for ourselves and mostly for our horses. Would you deny us those things, and be careful now Mr. King because your answer will tell me a whole lot about your intentions."

"No sir. We would not deny you re-provisioning. You may water your horses, get more water for your bags which I see are almost empty, and you may, if you wish, stay the night, rest up, have something to eat and buy whatever you need for food to continue your journey. Calipatria is about ten to fifteen miles from El Centro. We don't care what you do there. There is no sheriff there and no law there. You will be on your own when you get there, but by God you will not shoot our town up. Now pass the guns to us please. You will receive a receipt for them at the Sheriff's Office."

Ross nodded to Ralph and each of them in turn gave up their guns to the deputy, with their holsters and scabbards since it would make them easier to identify when the time came. Ross was the last of them to do so. When he was done he said to the deputy, "Where's my receipt?"

The deputy answered, "We are going to go to the sheriff's office right now and get one." Ross was a little concerned about it but didn't think it should be too much of a problem. It turned out to be fine. The sheriff, Joe Mullaney, greeted them, shook each of their hands in turn and when Manny was identified to him he said, "Young man if I had lost my wife and child in the way you have I would be out to gain revenge as well. I have every sympathy with you. My town has every sympathy with you. But this is 1910. And we do not resolve problems using guns any longer in this town. Mr. Martin is not here and he won't be here ever again other than passing through if I have anything to say about it. I consider him just as much a piece of human waste as you do Mr. Hendershot. But he will not be gunned down on my streets either."

The sheriff turned back to Ralph and Ross at one point and said to them, "You men have reputations which preceded you many years ago. I am sorry we felt it necessary to intercept you in this fashion. We simply could not allow gunplay on our streets. We will hold your weapons until you leave. When will you be going, do you know?"

Ross said, "About 5:30 a.m. tomorrow morning. Do you have anyone who rises early enough to let us in or will we have to kick in the door of your office?"

He was not being a smart aleck. Everyone could see when he said he would kick in the door to get his weapons he meant every word. The sheriff saw it as well. He added, "One thing Sheriff, if you knew our reputations why did you deem it necessary to treat us as a group of outlaws, putting fifty men in our way. I tell you this. If we thought for one moment you were harboring Martin here we would have killed all your men and had no qualms about it. Your knowing of who we are should have told you enough to know we were not a threat to your town if Martin was not here."

The sheriff responded, "I'm sorry, did my deputy not make it clear to you right away Martin was not in our town?" Mullaney glanced at King for a moment as he asked the question.

Ross, shaking his head vigorously, said, "No, he did not. Because of his tardiness in telling us Martin was not here he damn near provoked my son into shooting him first. I am afraid if my son had been armed Mr. King would be dead."

Mullaney countered by saying "Fortunately nothing happened which could not be controlled, Mr. Hendershot. It is a disappointment to me and I apologize to you insofar as my deputy did not tell you of Martin being in Calipatria in a more timely way. I promise you I will speak to him of his oversight and the potential trouble it could have created. As to the time of day you choose to leave I would expect nothing less than you would be an early riser. My deputy here, Shamus, will be here when you arrive. If he is not here then I give you leave to kick in the door. Your weapons will be stacked right here where they are now. No one will touch any of them in any way."

"Who will protect them and see to it that no one steals them?" This was, Ross thought, even as he said the words, probably unnecessary. It was another way he could voice his displeasure at the way he and the rest were treated by King. He added, to take the sting out of the possibility the sheriff would feel an insult had been hurled at him, "I am an older man now Sheriff. I am still alive though and I would not suffer the loss of any of these weapons well."

"We have a man who sleeps in the back room of the jail who is a deputy as well. He is armed and would stop anyone from taking the weapons. Is he enough to allay your concerns?"

"What do you say to the idea one of the four of us stays the night with these weapons so we can see to it ourselves they are being protected?"

The sheriff smiled, scratched his chin a little and then responded, "You would be locked in. The door will be locked at around ten o' clock tonight and it is stout so no one would break it down easily Mr. Hendershot. It is also locked from the outside so no one on the inside could simply take the guns and walk out."

"Even so sheriff, I would prefer one of us stays with the weapons if it is agreeable to you. They will be indispensable to us in capturing Mr. Martin in order to bring him back to Yuma for trial. Rest assured, by the way, our intent is fully to capture him and bring him back to Yuma for trial."

"Is that your real intent here Mr. Hendershot?" The sheriff directed his question to Manny this time, looking directly into Manny's eyes for his answer. It was clear this was a challenge.

Manny was up to the challenge for sure. He had considered the notions surrounding the taking of revenge for four days on the trail. His mind was made up. "Sheriff, if I had my way I would string the son-of-a-bitch up to the nearest tree I could find to where he is currently located. But sheriff, in answer to your question capturing him and taking him back to Yuma for trial is exactly what I have in mind. I have given my word to my father I will not just gun the bastard down and if there is any man on earth I would not lie to it is my father for sure."

The sheriff could see the sincerity in Manny's eyes. Manny didn't blink at all when he followed up by saying, "But don't get me wrong. If he tries to fight us, if the whole goddamned town of Calipatria tries to fight us, he will die and every man there will die as well. Hearing those words, the Sheriff thought, my goodness there is real metal is this young man.

The sheriff nodded, looked at Ross and said "If you want someone here we can arrange a bed for you in the nearest cell to the inner door. The door to the jail will be locked. No one in this town would dare to try and get in here. But if you think it necessary we can do it."

Jonas, who had remained very quiet though the entire ordeal of the deputy coming out to meet them and the escort into town as well as the conversations with the sheriff, said, "I will be the one to stay, Dad," he said to Ralph, "And Ross, you two and Dad need the rest more than any of us tonight. Go and find yourself a hotel. Bring me something back to eat. I will stay here and sleep here when they lock it up."

Ross, Manny and Ralph were directed to a livery, paid a fee to have the horses washed down, rubbed down, cleaned up a little and fed some hay and some grain. Water was available to them and they drank freely while the men were paying the fees. They found there was a hotel and saloon down the street and there was a cafe a little further away as well. They ate, took food to Jonas and went to the hotel where they all cleaned up, brushed the dust off their clothes and all were in bed asleep before nine o' clock in the night. All anticipated a difficult day to come. Their dreams were fitful at best. Manny's dreams were repetitive, making him relive the sound of the shot, the death in his wife's eyes, the horror of knowing she had flown away from him.

Ross awoke first at about the same time he always awoke, somewhere earlier than five in the morning. He rousted the others, got them going and they went to the cafe where they found hot coffee. There were some sweet kind of roll like things the cafe had made as well and they took some of those and went directly to the jail.

At the jail, which was already open, they found deputy Shamus King and Jonas. Jonas had already put his gun back on his body and was ready to go to the horses right away. They all strapped on their weapons and left the Sheriff's Office to go to the livery escorted by the deputy. After they saddled and bridled the horses they mounted and rode away with deputy King showing them the direction in which they must travel.

He said to them before they left, "Martin's mother is a whore who works in Calipatria servicing the miners. Because she sees to their needs they are friendly to her and to him. You may encounter some trouble either on the trip there or after you have gotten there with some of those men. Beware. They are hard men and will not hesitate to kill you given the opportunity."

Ralph muttered "Much obliged," as the four rode away. It was all the thanks he could muster up after the way things had gone down the day before. Deputy King just nodded, turned and walked away with a "Good luck" said, with a sneer, and under his breath, "you will need it."

Manny was closest to King and heard the under the breath comment of good luck. Manny said, as they rode away, "We make our own luck, deputy." King turned and looked back at Manny who had already ridden away. King thought to himself he had made a life-long enemy in Manny Hendershot. He wondered what it would mean if they ever met again. He knew one thing, staring into Manny's eyes the day before, when Manny told him to go for it, he saw death. He saw swift, certain death in those dark eyes and he wanted nothing to do with it.

Ross said to the others as they rode out of El Centro, "If ever I propose to ride to this god forsaken piece of shit town again someone remind me of what happened here yesterday and this morning. What a bunch of idiots there are in this town. It reminds me of a herd of rabbits being chased by a good hunting dog. They circled the wagons and antagonized the wrong side of this situation. Not a good deal man."

Manny, hardly ever a mean-spirited man, hardly ever critical of sheriffs or their deputies, said, "Deputy King can count his lucky stars he is still alive. I seriously wanted to kill the bastard yesterday and would have if I had been wearing a gun. It was a good thing you took mine Dad."

Ross said nothing. He had seen the truth of what Manny said on the previous day. Ross thought, just as King did, the deputy had a brush with death which he was most fortunate to survive.

8

Manny, The Man in Charge

Mid-November 1910

The four talked before going into El Centro about Manny going without a gun on him on the way to Calipatria. He was not armed when they went to El Centro, and he surprised all of them a lot when he announced to the sheriff his purpose for being in California was to capture Martin, bring him back to Yuma and put him on trial for the murder of Janie and their unborn child. He also surprised them with the vehemence of his dislike for deputy King. It was uncharacteristic of him to direct so much anger at one person.

When they rode out of El Centro near 5:30 in the morning Manny wore his pistol. Though they had talked about the issue of his being armed previously there was such a bond of trust between all of them after his talk with the sheriff of El Centro none of them asked him to go to Calipatria unarmed again. In the lead of their queue of riders as they trotted out of El Centro was Manny Hendershot. He was Ross Hendershot's son through and through, and Ross could not be prouder of him. Though Manny was barely nineteen years old he had grown to be a true man in the last several days.

The four kept the horses at a trot for several miles as they left El Centro. The cool morning hours enabled the horses to withstand the work without much of a problem. After an hour or so of riding the horses began to lather a little and the four began to slow down and take it easier. It was Manny who made the decision to slow down. Each of them, his father, his godfather, and his god-brother applauded him mentally. The horses were at the point where they had begun to sweat which meant they were using a lot of water.

The four men dismounted and walked alongside the horses for a time. As they walked they gave the horses some water from their hats, and they talked a little in the process. For the first time since they had started the trek across the desert Ross said to Manny, "What are your plans, son?", giving all the understanding of Manny now being completely in charge of the effort.

Manny responded, "I don't know yet Dad. I am a little worried we might run onto some of Martin's friends before we get to Calipatria. If I were Martin and I had heard we were coming, I might try to set up an ambush somewhere along the way for us. But this country is so flat and so barren and without natural cover I don't know how they could arrange an ambush yet. Maybe the terrain will change by the time we get closer to Calipatria, but I am thinking about the issue for a lot of reasons. One of those is what the sheriff told us in El Centro. Remember he said there is no 'law' out here."

Ralph chimed in then and said, "Maybe we should ride in twos, separately, and see if they really do know we are coming for him, and then if they try to set an ambush maybe we can at least make sure you and Ross get to Calipatria safely Manny."

What Ralph was saying to them all was he was willing to set himself up and Jonas with him to take the brunt of an attack by friends of Martin if one took place. Manny would have none of it. He said in response, "No, if any of us is going to get shot here today it will be me. This is my fight primarily and if they want to make it a fight then I will ask for your help for sure. I am very glad all of you are here but in the first place it will be me which leads us into whatever is going to come our way. Thank you, my Godfather, my second Dad, thank you very much. I know you want to help and you will, I have no doubt. But you also know this is primarily my fight."

Once again the pride swelled in Ross's chest. He said to them all, "Let's ride in slowly from here, give the terrain a very close eye all the time. I think we can rely on Jonas to give us an idea if it is changing enough to permit a group or even one man hiding out to try and shoot at us. With his experience I think we can probably get close to the town before anyone might try anything and then again if Martin is smart, which I doubt, maybe he will try to set something up as a greeting for us when we ride in there."

Jonas, whose life experience included scouting for the Army in the last couple of years of the Apache wars, said, "I'll ride at the point about a quarter mile or so ahead of the rest of you so I can give you a warning if I see anything which resembles a spot from which an ambush might be tried. My sense of Martin is he had enough guts to stand up to us. Of course, after shooting Janie in the back his attitude may have changed a great deal. He would be damned foolish if it had not changed frankly." Having said those things Jonas mounted his horse and took off at a trot to get a distance between him and the other three. Once he was about four hundred yards in front of the others he slowed to a walk, then stopped to await their continuing.

Now it was Ralph's turn to feel the swell of pride and love for his son and for the kind of man his son had become. My God, he thought, I can't have been responsible for the growth of a man of his caliber and stature but I sure am proud to be his father right at this moment. They all mounted then and began to walk their horses toward a place none of them had ever been and yet Ross and Ralph had been there, in the sense of the kind of place it was, on many past occasions, some of which involved gunfire. Ralph, then Ross pulled their Henry rifles out of their scabbards and made sure a round was in the chamber and the gun was ready to fire.

Each of them leaned their rifles against their thighs and pulled their pistols from the holsters, checking to see they had loads in all six cylinders of each gun, something they normally would not carry. Normally each of them would have five loads in their pistols with the hammer down on an empty cylinder. It was a time-honored means of avoiding an accidental discharge which could damage them or perhaps kill one of their horses. As each man, including Manny, checked their pistols and replaced them in their holsters, they contemplated the terrain in front of them and with knee signals sent their horses walking again.

The dust from the mining operation and the general activity taking place in the small town of Calipatria began to be evident a short time after the four separated. Jonas was on point, maybe a quarter to half a mile in front of the other three. Ross, Ralph and Manny were spread out, each at least twenty-five to thirty yards away from each other. Ross rode slowly, leading them now, with his Henry rifle held across his legs and against the saddle pommel as he rode. Ralph also rode with his rifle in hand. Manny did not have a rifle of his own but he rode with the Sharps his father had brought along in hand. If they were forced to dismount and use the rifles Manny would give the Sharps to Ross and take the Henry. Manny carried ammunition in his pockets for the Henry. Ross carried ammunition for both the Henry and the Sharps. Manny was happy not to be carrying cartridges for the Sharps. The cartridges for the rifle were long, thick and heavy. Ross didn't have a lot of ammunition for the Sharps. They all felt it was probably unnecessary, but decided to take a couple of dozen rounds along with the rifle just in case it was needed.

As Jonas rode in front of them he was ranging back and forth for at least a quarter mile in each direction crossing the track they were following to Calipatria. It gave him a sight line down the trail the other three did not have. As he rode across the trail, back and forth, he saw a wagon which looked like it was stopped alongside the trail some distance ahead of him. He could see it was a Conestoga type wagon, the same many pilgrims had used to travel westward in the last many years. He could also see the canvas top which normally would have shaded the occupants of the wagon was not up. The mules which were used to pull the wagon were not hooked up either. They were grazing maybe a hundred yards or so away from the wagon, and there did not seem to be any kind of a fire going next to the wagon as Jonas came nearer to it.

Jonas decided this was a strange kind of set up and shied back away from the situation to get a better look. He started to circle back away from the wagon toward the mules but extending the circle to remain at the edge of good and accurate rifle fire. As he did so he waved in the general direction of the rest of them and they stopped. He continued his crisscrossing of the trail but was essentially staying the same distance from the Conestoga wagon as he rode. It simply seemed strange to him and he did not want to get closer before he could see if there were people in the wagon.

As Jonas was circling away from the wagon Ross saw a puff of smoke from the side of the wagon and saw Jonas go down alongside his horse and take off at a gallop. They could see he was drawing his rifle from the scabbard as he ducked down on the opposite side of his horse from the side of the wagon from which it was now evident gunfire was coming. All of them could hear the rifle reports in the distance as Jonas rode in amongst the mules and stopped alongside one of them.

Jonas dismounted from his horse once he was amongst the mules. As he did Ross asked Manny to hand him the Sharps. Ross reckoned they were about five hundred yards away and maybe a little more from the wagon as he laid down in the dirt and extended the tripod on the Sharps. The three of them heard Jonas fire a couple of rounds in the direction of the wagon but could not hear if the rounds had any effect.

Ross could see Jonas clearly through the scope on the Sharps and he could see that Jonas was not wounded. He aimed at the wagon, about half way down the length of the wagon, loaded the buffalo gun and fired a round into the side of the wagon. Nothing happened. He fired a second and a third round into the side of the wagon and suddenly two men stood up in the wagon and threw their weapons over the side of the wagon onto the ground. Ross kept his eye on the two men in the wagon through the scope of the Sharps. He loaded another round into the gun to be able to fire, just in case the surrender was a ruse to draw one of them near only to be attacked once again.

Jonas mounted and rode toward the wagon with his rifle and his handgun at the ready. As he came within about twenty-five yards of the wagon he was holding the rifle in his left hand and his Peacemaker in his right. He put the rifle into the scabbard, occupying his right hand for a moment. As he put his rifle away, when he was not holding a gun directly on the men, one of the men dropped his hands quickly and drew a handgun, raising it to fire on Jonas. Ross had been watching through the scope, anticipating this kind of move. As the man reached for the handgun and started to bring it up a round which Ross had fired from the Sharps struck the guy in the middle of his chest.

The man's chest seemed to explode all over his buddy in a cascade of tiny drops of blood. This stupid man who had attempted to raise the handgun, humped over slightly, inclining his body toward the bottom of the wagon, and fell dead. The other man in the wagon seemed to try and raise his hands even higher than before. By then Jonas had arrived at the wagon, riding up alongside the man standing in the wagon and sapped him in the head. The guy was asleep in a moment but he was not injured.

Ross, Ralph and Manny went to the wagon at a gallop. Jonas waved at them it was okay and they slowed to a canter and then a walk as they neared the wagon. The old wagon was bare of any content save for the two shooters. As the second of the shooters awakened from his sap induced nap he was trussed up hands and feet and tied to one of the wheels of the wagon spread eagle. Jason had seen men placed in this position many times in the wars with the natives.

The natives would cut pieces off and otherwise torture a man placed in this position. Jonas had no intention of torturing the man but thought if he was convinced it might happen any conversation would be shortened. The warmth of the day had begun to creep up by the time this firefight was over and the man was placed on the wheel. As the shooter awakened a little water was splashed on his face. He was asked by Manny, "Do you want a drink of water sir?"

He answered "Oh yes sir, thank you kindly. I am kind of parched. We didn't think to bring a flagon of water with us. We were talking about riding back to town and getting some water when you all came along."

Manny gave the man a drink from one of their canteens. He was very grateful for the water and said, "Oh thanks so much, sir." He also said, "My name is Henry Little and I am from Calipatria. My buddy here in the wagon was Jimmy Jones. He is dead I reckon. Are you going to kill me too?"

"No Henry, we are not going to kill you. Do you want to die here today?" Manny asked.

"Well, no sir I reckon not but then hell any day is as good as any other, don'tcha think? I guess given the fact we tried to drygulch you men it might be something you would think about." Manny did not take Henry's comment as being smart alecky because the man was trussed up on the wagon wheel. Manny thought any man, no matter who it was, might have said what Henry did.

But Manny did not like his point of view. Manny said, in a deadly serious tone, "No Henry, I don't think any day is a good one. Now why don't you tell us why you two men set up an ambush out here for us? Did Robert Martin pay you to do that Henry, was that it?" Manny asked.

"Yes sir, it surely was the reason. We didn't have any other reason for sure. He gave us ten dollars apiece to try and shoot one or more of you men. I reckon it didn't work out so well seeing as how my bud is dead and all. Turns out we weren't so good with those rifles. You men were. But it was a day's work and I ain't had many of those since I got fired from the mine. Hell, I probably would have done it for five dollars. The mine didn't like it I was drinking too much one night and got in a fight the next morning with my shift foreman. They sent me packin. Man, oh man, what the hell did you shoot my pard with, sir, if you don't mind my asking sir."

"No, it's all right Henry, you can ask. It was a buffalo gun, a Sharps rifle." Manny took it out of Ross's scabbard and showed it to Henry. Then Manny asked Henry, "How many of Martin's pards are going to be willing to fight against this gun do you think Henry?"

Henry was not quick to answer but said, when he was ready, "Not many of them I would think, sir. The damned thing threw splinters all over us before my pard stood up and made his stupid play for his pistol. I was telling him we ought to give it up, we ought to tell you men whatever you wanted to know and go home. Ten bucks sure as hell was not worth our life, not in my view, but he was a stubborn cuss all his life, so it happened the way it did. I guess I should tell you there are more like us, many more to whom Martin has been giving money, or his whore has been servicing, who are willing to try and stop you from taking Martin. There are a bunch of them in the saloon in town right now wondering what happened out here. It's close enough to town to where you can hear the shots there, especially from the damned cannon you used to kill my pard. I would guess someone is going to come out here and take a look see soon."

About the time Henry ended his comments about the men in the saloon, there came a dust plume on the horizon. All of them could see the plume and knew it represented many more than just one man. Jonas, who had ridden on a way toward Calipatria, came running back on his horse as fast as he could. He slid to a halt, dropped the reins of the horse as he dismounted and said "I think we've got maybe fifteen or twenty minutes and I am guessing but from the dust plume and what I was able to see standing on top of my horse I would say there are about twenty of them. I couldn't tell for sure but it looked like Martin was in the lead group of them. There are two groups. One is coming fast and hard, the other is coming at a trot it looks like. But it could change any time I'm sure."

Henry Little chuckled a little and said, "Those ones who are a trottin on their horses won't have much stomach for a fight I would guess. After the first few rounds are fired they are going to high tail it back to Calipatria. But the ones in front are kinder like my pard here, a little stubborn, probably full of the booze like he was and willing to die to see what is going on out here for sure. Crazy thing is they don't know Martin much at all. He has been spending money though. Don't know where he is getting it because he sure as hell doesn't work. I would guess it is comin from his whore."

While Henry was talking Jonas was digging with one of his metal plates and creating a kind of berm. He said to Ross and the rest of them, "If you guys will get with it you have a little time to get one of these built too. I saw it done in the Army a lot and it saved a lot of lives." He got the berm about a foot high or a little less and ran around getting some big rocks and putting them in the face of the berm.

By the time Jonas was finished everyone else was doing the same thing. Ross put his little parapet right next to the wheel of the wagon that was facing to-ward the group which was riding hard at them. Ralph and Jonas were at the other end of the wagon. Manny stayed next to Ross. They could see all the riders. Ross took out the Sharps and looked through the scope. With Jonas' help he picked out Martin and let Martin get about two hundred yards away from the wagon before he shot the horse out from under Martin.

Before shooting Martin's horse out from under him Ross said to Manny, "I really don't want to kill a bunch of these men. If it becomes necessary I will Manny. I hope it will not be necessary. These men are just ordinary people who have chosen a friend and the friend is leading them astray. They don't deserve to die just for those reasons. Ross yelled at Jason and Ralph, before shooting Martin's horse, "Let me take the lead on this one and see what I can work out here."

Martin went down head first and his horse went down hard. It was evident right away either Martin was hurt or knocked out or maybe he was dead. Martin just laid there in the dirt. No one tried to pick him up and put him back on a horse. Several of the other riders behind Martin got tangled up in the situation of Martin's horse being shot and they fell as well. When the rest of the lead group were about a hundred yards away, still charging toward Ross and the others, Ross put another round into another horse which went down hard and again took two or three others with it.

One or two men came up with rifles and started shooting toward the wagon. Ralph shot one of them and the man went down and didn't move. The other one was shot by Ross. He flew backwards about a foot when the buffalo gun round hit him in center mass of the chest and he and the other rider died almost side by side.

The larger group of riders had stopped by the time the two men lay dead on the dirt. There was a lot of milling around among them, then one man jumped down and looked at both the men on the ground. Seeing they were dead he jumped back on his horse and broke out of the group, again charging at Ross and the others. He died within ten feet of the start of this charge, shot by Jonas. The smaller group, which had been about six or eight men, from which the three dead men had been shot, now broke and ran, or what was left of them broke and ran.

The larger group followed suit almost immediately. They were all shouting and waving rifles in the air and a few of them even fired shots into the air but none of them came any closer than the spot where Martin lay in the dirt, and Martin still was not moving when all the rest of them took off, some of them on foot.

A few horses were jostling around and against each other, their heads down and their reins on the ground. Jonas rode up to where Martin lay on the ground and began trussing Martin up. Manny rode up right behind Jonas. Manny had his pistol out and he was cussing a blue streak at Martin. The hammer was back on the pistol, and Manny was aiming it at

Martin. Jonas said to Manny, "You want to shoot him little brother? You go right ahead. But remember the promise you made to dad. If you shoot this bastard it will not go down easily with dad. He never has been one to suffer broken promises easily. Will you step back, take a moment to think, little brother, please. Just take a moment to breathe and think, Manny, please."

By the time Jonas was done talking to Manny both Ross and Ralph had ridden up to the two of them after roping one of the loose horses and leading it to where Manny and Jonas were located. Manny still had his pistol pointed at Martin as Ross and Ralph rode up. But in a sudden movement which told Ross his son had been practicing with the art of drawing and shooting, Manny holstered the gun, put the tie down on the hammer and sat there on his horse for a moment before he broke down crying. "Forgive me Janie," he said, "I just cannot shoot a man in cold blood. I want to honey. I want to make him pay for what he did to you, but I just cannot shoot him down in cold blood." Manny's crying continued during the time it took for Ross and Ralph to get Martin onto the horse and tie him down. No one said a word for a time. Manny got off his horse and took out a clean shirt from his saddlebags. He changed shirts, all the while leaking tears but not sobbing. He wiped his eyes and blew his nose with the dirty shirt and put it back into the saddle bags. Ralph said about the entire situation, "Well, it looks like Henry Little out there was right about most of those boys. None of them wanted to be around very long after the lead started flying for real." Nothing further was said by anyone for a time. It didn't seem necessary or appropriate to any of these hard, western men.

Eventually Manny walked over to his dad. He looked up at Ross and put his arms around him and hugged him. He said to Ross, "You have made me a better man than I thought I was Dad. Thank you. If it were not for you, and what Jonas told me I definitely would have killed him right here and right now." Ross nodded but said nothing.

Then Manny walked over to Jonas and took Jonas by the shoulders for a moment and then hugged Jonas too. He said, "Thanks my brother. Thanks for bringing me back to the world. I was gone from it for a second there. You are a good and smart man Jonas Forney. I am lucky and proud to have you as my brother. If we ever get into another one of these shenanigans I want you on my side for sure." He looked back at his Dad and smiled, then said, "You too Dad, and for sure you too Uncle Ralph. Damn your cannon is effective, Dad."

Then he walked to Ralph, who smiled knowingly at Manny. Manny smiled back and said, "Uncle Ralph, you have been involved in my life from the very first day. Thanks for always being there for me and thanks for helping my dad teach me blood on the ground doesn't resolve much at all. If you hadn't been there, all of you," Manny said then, "I would have cheerfully shot a piece of dog shit laying on the ground full of holes here today, but you were there, and if I shot him it would not do what I want to happen to this dog meat. I want him to be completely and utterly humiliated in front of the world for killing a young girl for no reason at all. So, let's get this dog shit back to Yuma so he can be hanged in front of a large crowd of people on the street. The four of them took the time before leaving the area to bury the three dead men and say some words over them. None of the four were religious men. But they believed in a God of some kind and wanted the souls of the departed to be given good treatment in the afterlife that all believed in. It was a small human gesture which all believed necessary. Ross and Ralph had done the same for desiccated bodies of men, regardless of their race or dress, when riding in the desert.

They rode back to the wagon where Henry was hanging on the wheel, let Henry loose and gave him a rope off the horse they had put Martin on to try and catch a horse before he got back to Calipatria. They let him drink some additional water, knowing they would be able to replenish their supply in El Centro.

Ross walked over to Henry and cut him loose. When he did he said to Henry, "Tell those men in Calipatria to stay where they are. We do not want any more gun play. We do not want to have to kill a bunch more of them. But by God you make it damn clear they know if they come within rifle range of us then some more of them will die swiftly. Can you tell them those things Henry?"

"Yes Sir. I certainly can do that. I seen you shoot with your damn blunderbuss and it ain't pretty to see a man die who is hit with it. I will be sure to tell them my feelings about seeing some of my friends shot too. Hendershot is your name isn't it?" "Yes, that is my name Henry. Tell them one more thing. This man murdered my son's wife and unborn child for no reason at all to do with my son. Robert Martin didn't have the balls to come looking for me. I killed Robert Martin's father many, many years ago when George Martin tried to shoot me. My son was not born at the time, and in fact not for many years afterward. George's brother came after me, tried to drygulch me in the desert and failed. I let him live despite his murderous intent. Ralph here shot William Martin dead in the streets of Yuma. Robert Martin didn't have the balls to come after Ralph either. Instead he came after my son and killed my son's wife and child, and rode away like the coward he is. If those men who joined him want more trouble over those facts of life all they must do is let me know. I am always available and my son can get word to me easily if someone from this town wants to challenge us to a gun battle. If so my son and I will come back to your town and kill every goddamned son-of-a-bitch in the town, one by one, including you. Do you hear me Henry?"

"Yes sir, Mr. Hendershot, I hear you and I believe you. I can see it in your eyes sir. No one will come against you from Calipatria again. You can be assured I am telling you the truth sir. I will make it clear what will happen if they do. Thank you, sir for letting me go. Can I get headed back to town now?"

"Sure Henry. Take off. Remember what I said though, every single man in the town will die if I see a face from there ever again."

After the four started their trek back to Yuma, taking Robert Martin with them, he began to awaken. He was very groggy at first because he had taken a blow to the head. He had a great deal of difficult understanding why his hands were tied behind him and his feet were tied together under the belly of the horse he was riding. As he gathered the wool in his head he began to cuss them, demanding to know what authority they had to take him, to truss him up and kidnap him. They provided no answers until Ross grew tired of Martin's ranting and said to him, "If you don't shut your mouth I am going to stuff a pair of dirty socks in it and tie a rope over it to keep it in place. Do you hear me Mr. Martin?" Martin grunted his understanding and became quiet. He finally realized what had happened and who it was talking to him. He said, "Are you Ross Hendershot?"

"Yes. I am Ross Hendershot. Now shut up." Martin finally became quiet. As they neared El Centro the sheriff and his deputy, this time by themselves, came out to escort them into town. "Hi men," the sheriff said. "I see you have Mr. Martin with you. What is your intention Mr. Hendershot?", the sheriff said speaking directly to Manny.

Manny looked at him for a moment, considering the situation completely, and said, "We still have some daylight to burn, sheriff. If we could stop and get some water and a little food to take on the rest of the trip we would be eternally grateful and then we will be out of your town for good. At least two of us will have to stay armed sheriff. To guard the prisoner sir, we will have to have two men guard him. By doing it with two men we will be able to give him some water and a bite to eat if he wants it without allowing him freedom of the use of his hands and feet."

Manny paused for a few moments, then said, "Perhaps you would like your deputy to stay with Ralph and Jonas. Or perhaps both of you would want to stay with them. In that way you can assure Mr. Martin comes to no harm in your town. If you wish to stay with Ralph and Jonas and if you would permit us the privilege the other two of us, my father and I, will go into the general store and get some food. Then we will want to use one of your pumps to fill our canteens and bladders. When we are done with those few things if you wish you can ride with us to the edge of town and give us our guns back. Will my suggestion work for you sheriff?"

"It certainly does son, and my congratulations to you Mr. Hendershot senior. You have raised a man of honor who also happens to be able to use his head for something besides a hat rack. We will do it just as you say Mr. Hendershot younger, just exactly as you say. Now if you two would please to hand over your guns." Ross and Manny disarmed and gave their weapons to the sheriff. Now comprised of a group of seven they all rode into town, the four, their prisoner and two lawmen. It was quite a sight when you got down to it, Ralph remarked to Jonas as they rode into town. They did their business just as Manny had described to the sheriff they would, got on their horses after giving them some water, including the horse ridden by Martin. He was fully aware and awake by the time the shopping and the filling of the water bags was done. They rode together to the eastern edge of the town where the sheriff gave Ross and Manny their weapons and wished them a safe and uneventful journey home.

Before the sheriff and Deputy King turned back toward El Centro Deputy King spoke directly to Manny. He said, "Mr. Hendershot, I am very sorry for your loss. I cannot imagine how you have borne this so well sir. I also want to apologize for my behavior the first moments of our meeting. I should have been much more tactful than I was. It was a good lesson to me, just as this apology has been. I hope you can accept my apology Mr. Hendershot."

Manny walked his horse to the side of King's horse and stuck out his hand. He said only one word, with tears running down his face again. "Thanks."

As the four turned to ride away with their prisoner Martin said to the sheriff, "Are you just going to let them take me back to Yuma?"

The sheriff replied, "Why do you ask Mr. Martin? Did you think for even a minute a murdering son-of-a-bitch such as yourself, a back-shooting polecat like you would deserve anything else? Did you want us to do some kind of court thing here in El Centro Mr. Martin? If you did you piece of dog shit you are going to be very disappointed. Have a nice hanging Mr. Martin. I hope the rope doesn't break and I hope rather than it breaking your neck when you fall you choke to death slowly. It is better than what you deserve you piece of shit. If it were up to me I would stake you out to an anthill like the Apaches."

The sheriff tipped his hat to the four and again bid them a safe journey. As they readied to leave Manny rode close to the sheriff and stuck out his hand and vigorously shook hands with both the sheriff and the deputy again, saying "Thank you, sheriff, you have been very fair with us and I appreciate it very much. Take good care now. I suppose I should mention we had a bit of trouble back there in Calipatria. Some of the locals thought it necessary to come at us with guns. It was a huge mistake on their part. We left three graves in the desert. We had captured a drygulcher named Henry Little but he didn't know their names so we left no markers on the graves. You were right sheriff, there was law in Calipatria.

9

The Ride Home to Yuma, A Trial, Revenge

Late November 1910

The four knew the trek home would be three to four days on the trail, knew there was little water on the trail and not much firewood. They stopped relatively early after leaving El Centro and began to gather what they could for firewood. It was difficult because there were not very many trees in the area. One part of the ride back was, as it had been on the way to El Centro, through a large set of shifting and sometimes very tall sand dunes. There was no vegetation around the dunes at all. The dunes were two days riding away from their first stop for the night. Between the dunes and the first night's stopping place there was little vegetation other than creosote bushes. Creosote did not burn well and it took way too much of it to make a fire. After the first night they would dry camp as they had going west.

Getting Martin set up so he could eat with them was a little tricky. He was not being cooperative at all even though he was not being vocally abrasive. Having received a beating at the hands of both Manny and Jonas he didn't want to create any more provocation than was already there, and the antipathy which already existed toward him was clearly very deep. He kept his mouth shut except when asked a question like, "Do you want some coffee Martin?" Then he answered yes or no but nothing more. To allow him to drink coffee or eat they tied his hands in front of him and tied them to a loop around his ankles as well.

Martin knew if he tried to escape these men would not hesitate to beat him or kill him if necessary. Even though his circumstances were clear he plotted, watched and waited, thought he might be able to get enough distance between him and the four if he were quiet in the night, but then they tied him up again. The ropes had been taken off as he came down from his horse, but when it came time for them to sleep he was tied up again, and as a part of being tied up he was tied to one of them. What a situation. It might be impossible for him to escape and what then? Would they hang him for killing that pretty little girl? He thought they probably would.

Thus, he laid quietly in the night, trying his best to loosen the ropes enough for him to slip out of them. The knots were not so tightly woven it was impossible, but it was difficult. He fell asleep. He was exhausted from riding with his hands tied behind him. It took every bit of his concentration to keep pressure of his knees on the horse and not fall off repeatedly. Riding and particularly falling off a horse was dangerous as well, especially because his feet were tied to each other with a rope draped across the bottom of the horse's belly. If he fell off he was very likely to get kicked in the head. No, the only way he would escape, if at all, was in the night when they were all asleep.

Ross had been a deputy sheriff when he was much younger. Ralph had been a constable, a deputy sheriff and a sheriff in various places including Yuma. The two of them had no intention of permitting Martin to escape. During the first evening before bedding down the two of them took a walk together. Ralph said, when they were well away from the camp, "He's going to try and get loose and get away. You know I'm right don't you, bud?"

Ross nodded his head and said, "Of course you are right Ralph. He has been working on the ropes around his hands since we left El Centro, but I think he cannot figure out what to do about the rope on his feet. You are right he will try and it will come in the night. One of us should doze and we will tie his leg to one of us after we eat. Maybe we should search him carefully and make sure he doesn't have a knife squirreled away somewhere." Up to then no one had bothered to search him beyond taking his guns away when they got him up out of the desert near Calipatria.

They searched Martin and found a small knife in his boot in a small pocket which could be used for a knife or a pistol. It was not big but it could have been used to cut ropes if he had gotten it out. Ralph, when he found the knife, said to Martin, "This really is disappointing Mr. Martin. I was hoping you would have a hideout gun in there and try and get it out in camp one of these evenings. But this little knife couldn't cut butter. What were you going to do with this, skin a quail or something?" Ralph laughed at Martin as he walked away. He threw the knife into the desert the next morning as they went on.

The ride the second day turned into a nasty one because of a wind storm. They were passing through an area of dunes and when the wind started to blow the sand was carried into the air. It felt like bees stinging as it hit exposed skin. Each of the four, in turn, covered up with whatever they had available, bandannas, extra shirts, anything to keep the sand off their skins. Manny, of all the people to be willing to do so, covered Martin's skin as well as his own. It was amazing to the other three to see Manny tending to Martin, covering him against the sand. Martin said nothing while Manny was seeing to his needs.

The wind storm lasted for several hours. It finally got so bad, visibility was so low they huddled the horses together with themselves and tried to stand in circle which would protect them all with their backs to the wind coming from the west. As they did Martin had a momentary chance to be free from the ropes on his feet and he ran off into the dust. Within seconds he was out of sight and gone. The four knew they could never find him in the storm so they stayed put where they were while the wind and sand raged around them. They all knew there would be time enough to look for him when the storm was over. He would not get far.

When the stinging sand and the wind driving it had abated a little they mounted up, began to circle and search for Martin. They found him laying on the ground maybe one hundred yards from where he had run off. They laughed at him and ridiculed him over his arrogance. They scoffed at the notion he might have had, thinking even for a moment he could get anywhere in the storm. They tied him back on his horse, gave him a drink of water and headed east again. It was a moment which would eventually become a joke amongst the four and in time with a lot of their friends in Yuma.

The ride took three days. It was without further incident as to Martin. He apparently had become reconciled with the notion he was not going to escape. There were no other incidents of any kind with any others. Their progress was steady, plodding along in the dust, thinking of how wonderful a cold beer was going to taste when they got to the Palace. When they sighted the dust, plume surrounding Yuma and its area, Martin said, "What are you going to do, take me back and hang me today?"

Ross answered, "No, no Mr. Martin. We are not going to hang you at all even though it is what you deserve you dog shit. If you hang it will be at the hands of the Territory of Arizona and the law, not at our hands. We are going to deliver you to the sheriff and he is going to put you into the Territorial Prison until a judge can be brought to Yuma for your trial." They camped one last night before going on into Yuma. They could see the lights of the town as they sat around their campfire, small though it was. All had their own thoughts about returning, and mostly all were happy to be going home.

Ralph had been very quiet during the entire trip to and from Calipatria. The last night on the trail before arriving in Yuma he wanted to talk to Manny and he wanted Martin to hear what he had to say. After they all had eaten a little pemmican and the last of the hardtack Ralph said to Manny, "I need to get something off my mind Manny. So here goes. A lot of years ago now, over twenty years ago, my daughter's horse came running into my little ranch without my daughter. I jumped on the horse and went looking for her." Ralph choked a little for a moment, stopping to take care of some tears and blow his nose.

Jonas put his head down and shook it. He thought he knew what Ralph wanted to say. He put his hand on his father's shoulder, and said, "Take your time, Dad. It's been a long time this has needed to come out." Ralph looked at Jonas for a moment, thinking to himself, how can he know this, and then answering his own question with a mental acknowledgement, he is my son, he knows me better than I thought.

Ralph continued and said, "Manny I saw your eyes when you were holding on the asshole over there, son. I saw the look in your eyes. I saw the determination in your eyes to kill him, to rid the earth of his brand of scum. I am so proud of you, just as is Ross, you didn't do it, you didn't just blow his ass into a pile of dirt. I know the very thought you held Manny, I know it all too well. I stood in front of Jason Grant with a shotgun loaded with double ought buckshot ready to kill him for good, but I didn't do it either. And after all these years I think now I know why. Excuse me for a moment."

Ralph walked away from the campsite for a few minutes, blew his nose again, cleaned the tears up again and then returned. "I'm getting to be an old man, son and my Jennie has been gone for many years, but when I looked at that piece of dog meat who raped and killed my daughter I was not an old man. Oh my God help me I wanted to kill him just as badly as you wanted to kill this dog shit over here a couple of days ago. Once again, I didn't, and you didn't. There is a difference in us, in you, in me, in Ross, in Jonas from this bag of shit. He never knew himself, never knew his parents, never knew how to be a man. He thought the vendetta he went on against you made him a man. In the end all it made him is a murderer, and you are not a murderer Manny. None of us are murderers. There is the difference between you and Martin, and it was the same difference between me and Jason Grant. So tomorrow when we go home to Yuma you can hold your head high, and you can go and get drunk if you want to. Give booze a little time if you want, if you have need. I did for sure. Ross helped me out of those times. Jonas will help you out of it when you are ready, or for sure you know Ross and I are here for you as well."

Manny was crying hard by then. Ralph knew he had to break through, to make Manny understand it was all right for him to go on and live the rest of his life, it was not right for Janie to be gone, but it was all right for him to continue. Ralph knew well the desire Manny had to die at the moment of Janie's death, and for the entire trek to Calipatria and back. "Manny my godson, you are as much kin to me as there is on this earth just as Jonas is the same with Ross. Your old man and I are like brothers born under different roofs. I know you, son because I know your dad and I know me. You must live now, son. Get drunk for a while if you must, or throw yourself into making the business even more successful than it has ever been, but you must live. You must live to understand, as you will in time Janie would want you to live, not die. She had her life ended by a pile of shit. Your life is just starting. Yes, it will be very hard for you to go on every day, and some days will be a lot harder than others. Yes, you will want to kill yourself just as badly as you wanted to kill Mr. dog shit Martin, but you must live. You must live for you, for what may come your way in the future, for all you can do to help others in this life. You must live Manny."

Ralph took Manny in his arms. Manny was sobbing. He seemed almost inconsolable. Ralph held him for a few minutes. Then Ross stood and held Manny for a long time. For the first time in many years Jonas and Ralph hugged each other after he stepped away from Manny. Martin who had watched all this knowing he must not say anything made the mistake of thinking the main thrust of Ralph's comments was over and they would soon sit down around the fire again. Martin muttered something about the love fest being over.

Manny heard him. He stepped back from Ross and looked at Martin. He said, "No Dad, it's all right. I won't kill him. He deserves it every second he lives but I won't be the one to do it." He walked over to Martin and said "Keep your trap shut you fucking piece of dog shit or I will put you between the horses and let them pull your arms and legs off you. Don't speak another fucking word, do you understand me?" Then he kicked Martin in the guts, doubling Martin over on the ground where he laid out retching.

Martin made no sound he had heard Manny or recognized the threat Manny had made was real. It was a
mistake for which he paid with pain. Manny walked
to him again and said, "I asked if you heard me you
piece of shit?" He kicked Martin in the guts again. As
he retched again Martin nodded at Manny and put his
hands up to indicate he understood.

Manny walked over to Ralph and Jonas and said
to Jonas, grasping him by the shoulders, "Thank you,
my brother. You have kept me from killing myself
since the day Janie died. I wanted to die. You know I
wanted to die but you saw to it I lived. Thank you, my
second father Ralph. You are right, I may get drunk,
but I know my brother will be there to help if need be
and he will get me out of the drunkenness when he
thinks the time is right if I cannot make the choice
to come out myself."

He hugged Ralph and looked him in the eyes and
said "I am so sorry you had to go through all the pain
I know you felt. I know it was the hardest thing you
have ever had to do because this is most certainly the
hardest thing I have ever done. I love you all for being
here, for being here for me to support me when I need
it the most. It will take a little time but I will live and
I will be back into the business again. I promise it to
all of you."

10

An Ending, Drunkenness, Peace

December 1910

It took a while for a circuit judge to get to Yuma for the trial of Robert Martin. There was a judge in Yuma who could have done the job but he said he had to stay out of it because he knew and loved Janie too much. He called it recusing himself and said it was a necessary thing when a judge knew someone involved in a case so well.

It had been a strange thing, coming back to Yuma with Martin lashed down to his horse, trussed up for the law to take charge of, hopefully to hang. Ross and Ralph had been involved in gunfights in the town, had rid the town and its businessmen of a shark named George Bonhomme, and had been lauded by a lot of people resultant to their past exploits in the town. They had never been cheered before.

Someone must have gotten word into the town the men were returning and were bringing Martin back to be tried in Yuma. People lined the streets. Business people shut their doors for a time, schools seemed to have let their children out of classes, the women came out from their chores of whatever nature. As the four men rode into town and toward the sheriff's office the people began to cheer, to root the men on, to say things like "Hang the Bastard." None of them had ever seen the like of this kind of behavior before.

The circuit rider was a traveling judge appointed by the territorial governor to take care of cases such as Martin's case. His name was Bret Stanley. Later he would move to Yuma and become one of the town's upstanding citizens. He always told people in later years it was the people of Yuma he came to respect and love in the Martin trial. It was his impetus to move there. He came to Yuma and took up residence in a private home. He didn't want to give the appearance of a conflict of interest by taking a room in the only hotel which he would think of engaging, it being the Palace.

The preliminary matters in the case were handled by Judge Stanley quickly. There was a motion to dismiss the case because of the kidnapping, as the lawyer called it in court, of his client in California and the false imprisonment of Robert Martin by a group of thugs, returning him to Yuma. All four men, Ralph, Ross, Manny and Jonas were forced to testify in the hearing. The defense lawyer was all sound and fury and nothing was accomplished by any of his tactics. A trial date was set, then postponed for several weeks.

It took a long time to choose a jury in Martin's case. Martin had a lawyer who insisted things had to be done the right way. Anyone who had known Janie well would not be permitted to sit on the jury or at least it was what Martin's lawyer wanted. After several weeks of wrangling and haggling between the defense lawyer, the town attorney and the judge there was a trial. It was a sensational day when it began, to be sure.

There were lots of drummers in the town with their wagons set up in odd places. They sold every product one could imagine. The barking announcements they made at least once every hour created a cacophony of sound near the courthouse. There was a small kind of circus which was there with a hand cranked calliope playing fun songs while the children danced around it with clowns. It really was not what Manny wanted. He wanted the trial to be deadly serious, for Martin to be convicted and hanged as quickly as the judge thought appropriate. Manny shook his head at the barking drummers and the hawking sales people. He thought the entire atmosphere was being ruined by their presence and their activities.

The townspeople of Yuma were abuzz with the trial and before it happened there were all kinds of rumors about whether Martin really was the guy who did the shooting, whether if he was found guilty, and surely he would be wouldn't he, would he hang? If he was to hang when would it happen? There was no one who was taking any bets. No one dared buck the odds as to he would be found guilty and hang. There was also a lot of gossip about the jury. Many of the jurors selected for the trial were brand new residents of Yuma and they had no knowledge of who Janie was, or what had happened.

The trial began with a lot of bluster and bravado by the town attorney and even more from the defense lawyer. The defense lawyer talked about how the only witnesses to the shooting were the "boy" Manny Hendershot and the sheriff, James Royal, and how neither one of them could identify the shooter. No one paid the defense lawyer much mind except for Ralph and Ross, Jonas and Manny. Ralph and Ross stayed on for the trial. Carmelita and Flora were there as well having left their ranches in the hands of the foremen for the time being.

Manny was the first witness for the town attorney. He hated the notion of having to relive the shooting by talking about the event. He railed a lot, in his cups on the eve of having to testify, about how he would be forced to deal with her death while looking a pile of shit in the eyes. He also knew for certain if he did not testify there was a possibility Martin would walk, not be punished at all. He would tough through it, he would be disgusted having to look Martin in the face, but he would do what was necessary.

When Manny was called to the stand and sworn in he was first asked some general questions, then he was asked about his and Janie walking on the day she was shot. He described how he and Janie took "constitutionals" together after her announcement she was pregnant and how they had walked together in the same fashion prior to her becoming pregnant nearly every day since their marriage. He described how Martin had come to the Palace and threatened him and how he had given Martin a beating and sent him on his way.

Then, under the gentle questioning of the town attorney, Manny described the shooting, what he had seen, and who he had seen. He described Martin, the way he had been dressed, and said he was virtually certain it was Martin who did the shooting. He showed no doubt and when asked to do so he pointed out Martin as the person who shot his wife and ran away.

When the defense lawyer got to cross examine Manny he apologized to him first for the shooting of his wife and her death as well as that of the unborn child. The lawyer did not ask about what happened, meaning how Manny held Janie in his arms as she and his unborn child died. At least he gave Manny a little space within which to deal with his questions. Then he asked what appeared to Manny to be the crux of his questioning, which was, "Did you see Mr. Martin's face the day she was shot?" Manny, always honest to a fault, said, "No sir, no I did not. I was more concerned about what had happened to my wife than I was about who had done it."

The attorney once again apologized for having to ask the next question but then asked Manny, "You have said you are virtually certain it was Mr. Martin. But you did not see his face. What was it which made you so certain Mr. Hendershot?" "The total circumstance, sir. He threatened me and all, then she was dead." It appeared as though Manny remembered something else as he raised his finger and said, "And there is one more thing, the sheriff saw Martin running away and then riding away."

The lawyer for Martin objected to what Manny said as being hearsay testimony and the judge said to Manny, "Just talk about what you know son, not what others have said."

"Yes sir. I'm sorry." The lawyer for Martin announced he was done with Manny and the town attorney did a little of what he called rehabilitation in conversation with Manny after the trial. He asked Manny, "How many other people were there on the streets when this horrid event occurred?" Manny said, "None which I saw." Manny understood what the defense attorney had done. He tried to be as positive as he could but the feeling he had after testifying was he should have lied and said he saw Martin's face. Then he knew in his heart of hearts it was not what Janie would have wanted.

The lawyer asked Manny to describe Martin as he had been seen on the day of the shooting. Manny responded with the same description he had offered earlier. Then the lawyer for the town asked whether he had any doubt in his mind about whether it was Martin or not? The answer was a resounding "NO!"

The town lawyer then dismissed Manny and called his next witness who was the sheriff. The sheriff was sworn to tell the truth by the judge and sat down next to the judge. The town attorney asked him, eventually, what he had seen the day the Janie Hendershot was killed. The sheriff answered, "I heard a shot, then another, and I was out the door of my office. I saw Manny and Janie down on the boardwalk and I ran toward them. As I ran toward them I saw Robert Martin running down an alley, mounting his horse and riding away." The defense attorney asked the sheriff only a few questions. His first question was "Did you see Mr. Martin fire a gun, sheriff?"

"No, I cannot say I did."

"Did you see Mr. Martin carrying a gun sheriff?"

"No, I cannot say I did."

"What was your primary concern at the moment you saw Manny and Janie on the ground?"

"To find out what happened."

"What did Manny tell you had happened?"

"He said someone shot Janie and me. It was kind of hard to understand what he was saying because Janie was already dead and he was crying and sobbing a lot. But I think he told me,"Someone shot Janie and me and ran off down the alley. I think it was Robert Martin."

The defense lawyer didn't ask anything else. The town attorney asked the sheriff one more set of questions. "Sheriff did you see anyone else running near where Janie and Manny were shot?"

"No, I did not."

"Sheriff did you see anyone else running down the alley besides Robert Martin?"

"No, I did not."

"Were you aware of the threats Robert Martin had made on the life of Manny Hendershot, sheriff?"

"Yes, I was."

"How long after those threats did this shooting occur?"

"Not long at all, a few days maybe."

"Sheriff, how did Janie Hendershot die, was it of old age, natural causes, an accident or a murder?"

"Janie was murdered in cold blood by a son-of-a-bitch…" He didn't get the rest of it out before the defense lawyer was on his feet yelling his objection to the reference to his client. The judge was banging his gavel, there was a lot of yelling going on and then suddenly it was over. The judge sent the jury, twelve men from the town, to a separate room which had been prepared for them at the back of the general store to see if they could arrive at a verdict of guilty or not guilty of the murder of Janie Hendershot. Everyone expected the jury would be out in deliberations for a few minutes and probably not more and then they would come back with a guilty verdict.

At the end of the day the jurors were not done. They were not done by noon the next day. The judge sent them home with instructions to take the day off and come back fresh the next day. They did but it didn't make any difference. One guy was hanging the jury up, and the rest of the jurors could not budge him from saying the town attorney didn't prove it was Martin who had done the shooting. The judge had no choice but to let the jury go and try to get another as soon as possible, but it didn't seem very likely he could get twelve men in the town who didn't know Janie or Manny, and didn't have an opinion already formed about Martin being guilty.

But the judge soldiered on, fought through the obstruction of the defense and got another jury sitting in the courtroom. The second trial went just the same way as the first, and the second jury hung up in the same way, with eleven voting for conviction and one for acquittal. They didn't want to let Martin go, most of them anyway, but they could not say it was him who did it for sure. All of them felt if they could not say it was Martin, definitively, they didn't want him to hang.

A week later, after trying get another jury sitting and failing, the judge let Martin walk. He had no choice he said. The law required him to let the defendant go because a jury could not convict him of the crime with which he was accused. Manny, Ross, Ralph and Jonas sat in the Palace Hotel and Saloon and wondered what the hell had gone wrong. They cussed it, discussed it for hours on end and concluded it was hard for a jury to see what had happened. None of them felt any rancor or anger toward the jurors. It was, after seeing the trial twice, even in Manny's eyes, a difficult thing.

The prosecutor didn't have an eye witness other than the sheriff and Manny who could say they saw Martin's face, saw him shoot, saw him with the gun. Manny understood even though it was not what he wanted, not what he knew was the right thing in his heart. The jurors didn't see the man with the gun shoot Janie in the back. There was no one to blame for the jury's decision. They had done an honest job and one juror just could not be persuaded he wanted to hang a man based on the testimony.

Ross and Ralph went to James Royal after the second trial ran down to an end, while the jury was out, and Ross said to him, "Sheriff, if this case gets hung up for good, Martin is such an idiot is likely to think he has free rein to come after my son. When Ralph and I were running the hotel, we were deputized in a way which made it possible for us to wear guns. Can you do the same for my son and Ralph's son Jonas? Of course, it would only be inside the hotel and saloon, and they would take them off whenever they went outside the building."

The sheriff was a prudent man and he could see the sense in what Ross was asking him to allow. He told Ross and Ralph he would think it over and put a plan into effect right after the trial was over. When the last attempt to obtain a jury was being made by the judge James Royal came to Manny and Jonas at the Palace and sitting down with the two of them when he told them he had a very serious matter to talk about, he said to them, "It may happen Martin comes after you again Manny. If the trial ends in a hung jury again he may feel like he has a free rein to do so. He is such an arrogant ass I am fearful he will take the wrong notions from a second hung jury. If it becomes necessary I don't want you to be unable to defend yourselves. I am authorizing you and Jonas to carry a pistol here in the Palace. Here," he said, handing them each a piece of paper which was an instruction to "All" giving them license to carry firearms inside the premises of the Palace, "I do not want to see you wearing a gun outside the Palace. Do both of you understand what I am doing here?"

Both Manny and Jonas realized the sheriff was doing them a favor, trying to protect them from the potential of another shooting. They also knew Martin was arrogant enough to try and pull off another killing since he probably thought he had gotten away with the first one. All the longtime residents of the town were highly miffed about the outcome of the two trials. Everyone knew it had been Martin who killed Janie. Just the fact that he ran, left town immediately and hid out in Calipatria was proof enough for most. It was not for at least one juror in each of the trials. The judge was quite strict in his instructions to all the jurors they should not disclose who had been the obstructionist. No one wanted another shooting.

Martin had stayed at the Cactus getting very drunk since the ending of the second trial. He was like a celebrity among some of those who had been his friends in the past. Many of them hated the Palace and everyone associated with it though none would be likely to be able to explain. No one would allow him to buy a drink. One of those who was buying slipped him a gun.

He hid it away in his coat when it was given to him. The guy who gave it to him told him he should go and finish the job he had started with Janie. Martin never did know who it was he talked to and gave him the gun. In the aftermath of what happened later no one ever could quite figure out who the person was. All they could say was he was tall and rangy.

In the end Martin finally consumed enough liquid courage to leave the Cactus. No one followed him. No one went with him. Martin didn't quite understand what he was doing in the first instance but he thought he was going the right direction for whatever it was he was going to do. He was a little confused about his vendetta. He didn't know whether Ross Hendershot or Manny Hendershot was the person he wanted to kill. Oh well, he thought, I'll just kill them both. Off into the night he went.

It was late. There were no more customers in the Palace. Jake was finishing his clean up routine behind the bar, washing dishes, glasses and getting the area cleaned up good and ready for the next day. Manny had gone into the hotel to check on how many rooms were full. It was becoming a residence hotel as much as anything. The men staying there tended to be there for weeks or months, generally as long as the jobs they were working lasted. Jonas was in the bar making a cash set up for Jake to use the next morning and getting ready to put a deposit together for the bank which would also be made the following morning.

The doors of the Palace were batwing, opening onto the street, not unlike thousands of other saloons across the country. As Martin slammed those doors inward and entered the saloon he saw Jonas, raised his gun and fired at Jonas, leaving the doors swinging back and forth. Jonas went to the floor and pulled his pistol, started to stand when he saw Manny come through the hotel passage saying, "No Jonas, no, this is my job."

Manny had a pistol in his hand. Martin heard him, looked in his direction and fired at Manny. Martin missed and died. Manny simply walked forward as Martin was firing, raised his pistol and shot Martin in the chest six times. Martin was dead before he ever slumped to the floor, still holding his gun in his hand. Jake, behind the bar, who had seen Ross Hendershot do much the same thing, many years earlier, said "Sweet Jesus you are the incarnation of your father."

Manny turned and looked at Jake and quietly asked Jake, "Would you please see to it the sheriff is told what happened here Jake, and would you please see to it someone goes and gets the undertaker and he gets this piece of shit out of here before he begins to stink up the place. Oh, and one more thing, there will be a lot of cleaning of the blood to be done. Will you see to it as well please? Now if you don't mind would you pour me a nice big drink and a cold beer?" Manny turned to his brother, Jonas who was standing behind the bar looking at Manny with eyes which said, I never have truly known you, have I. Manny asked, "Would you like one my brother?" Jonas was completely in awe of what had just happened. He had never seen a man face down another with guns in hand before. All the gun battles he had ever seen, either with the Army or with the four in Calipatria, were at long range with rifles. He certainly never had seen his little brother act as he had that night. "Yes, Manny, yes, I would," he said.

The two of them had not finished their beer and glasses of whiskey before the rest of the family, the sheriff and the undertaker arrived in the saloon from their various locations. Flora asked Jake to explain what had happened. Jake crossed himself and said, "Your son is an incredibly brave man." Jake described how it all came about to the entire crowd which had gathered around him when Flora asked her question.

Flora shook her head, grabbed hold of her man Ross and said "We are not needed here right now. I have not slept in the bed we are using in a long time and the last time we were here and in that bed, I didn't get much sleep. You better make sure it is true again tonight Mr. Hendershot." Ross nodded and off to bed they went on Christmas Eve Day, 1910 when Janie Hendershot was finally given her rest from the idiocy of Robert Martin.

About the Author

Berk Rourke was born in Douglas, Arizona on August 28, 1938. His careers were in teaching 8th and 9th grade students initially and then as an attorney for a total of some 40 years. He began writing as a cathartic exercise and enjoyed it so much that he continued with multiple efforts now being published for the first time. His life has known very few limits and his writing in at least two genres now has not known limits yet. Give it a look.

* * *

To learn more about H. Berkeley Rourke and discover more Next Chapter authors, visit our website at www.nextchapter.pub.

Revenge for Janie
ISBN: 978-4-82411-641-3 (Mass Market)

Published by
Next Chapter
1-60-20 Minami-Otsuka
170-0005 Toshima-Ku, Tokyo
+818035793528
17th December 2021